LIVING DEAD GIRL

Also by the Author:
Fake Liar Cheat

LIVING DEAD GIRL

a novel by

Tod Goldberg

SOHO

Published by
Soho Press Inc.
853 Broadway
New York, NY 10003

Library of Congress Cataloging-in-Publication Data
is available.

For Wendy, how do I explain the human heart?
All I know is that you are mine.

Among the scenes which are deeply impressed on my mind, none exceed in sublimity the primeval forests undefaced by the hand of man. No one can stand in these solitudes unmoved, and not feel that there is more in man than the mere breath of his body.

—Charles Darwin

LIVING DEAD GIRL

ONE

I AM HAUNTED by a memory I can't recall. How long has it been since the last time I was home? Five years? A week? How many days have I spent thinking about my children, thinking about time and consequence, when I should have been concentrating on today, tomorrow, on trying to become happy?

It is fall and the air is sharp. Ginny keeps telling me to slow down so that she can really "see" her surroundings. She wants to absorb this environment, smell the flowers and the weeds and the dead things on the side of the road. She wants to be able to re-create these things exactly.

Ginny wants to make films. She says she can see a screenplay unfolding every mile we drive.

She wants to be my wife. She wants to make me understand that there is artistry in my science.

Ginny is nineteen.

"Can we stop at the Krispy Kreme?" Ginny asks. "I've always heard wonderful things about their doughnuts."

I've already had a wife, a life; another existence separate from whatever Ginny is experiencing. She is beautiful, though. Her hair is long and blond, her stomach flat and tan. A ring dangles from her belly button and when we have sex she tells me to touch it. She tells me that the belly button is the beginning of life. I know that she is wrong. She tells me that she wants to have my baby, my babies, whatever.

I don't tell her what I want.

Leaves have already begun to litter the streets in gold and red, and when the wind picks up they dangle in the air and I think about how much that used to mean to me: The beginning and end of life. The change of seasons.

"You know they bake them fresh," Ginny says. We've pulled into the parking lot of Krispy Kreme. "Should we get a dozen?"

"No," I say. "You don't want to get sick on the lake."

Ginny leans over and squeezes my cheeks. She has an extra finger on her left hand. It's just a nub, really, beside her pinky. I noticed this the first day of class. She was sitting in the front row, drumming her fingers on the desk, and whenever I looked up from my lectern she was beaming at me with her twisted genetic code.

"I have sea legs," she says. "What about you, *Doctor?*"

I am not a doctor.

"Get half a dozen if they're hot," I say. "Otherwise we'll gorge ourselves."

While Ginny goes inside to order, I sit in the car. Granite City, Washington, was a logging town when we bought our house near here. Instead of the Krispy Kreme donuts, Blockbuster Videos, and Del Tacos that litter the streets now, there were bars and gun shops and two small grocery stores. We'd fallen in love with the slowness of it. She was going to raise our children at home, teach them from books that she thought meant something. No silly "Dick and Jane" books. She was going to teach them to read from Chaucer.

It was silly. It is silly.

We were going to bring them up as people. Teach them as we, humans, had been taught. No state-authorized curriculum.

If they were born with vestigial tails, they would keep them.

They would never be freaks because they would know that freaks are simply the misunderstood. They would understand everything.

Ginny and I have been driving for two days. We left Los Angeles on Thursday, wound through the Bay Area, spent an angry night screwing in Klamath Falls, and then climbed through Medford, Portland, and finally into Washington.

There used to be a small pond filled with goldfish where the Krispy Kreme is now. It wasn't the original pond, though. It was made of concrete and had a filtration system that preserved the ecosystem. It had been built on the soil of an actual "living" pond after Mt. St. Helens erupted and the ash had killed all of the fish and bugs that called the water home. There's a plaque now that tells the history of this parcel of land.

Ginny pops out of the doughnut shop, a doughnut stuffed into her mouth already.

"These are so good," Ginny says after she sits back down. "They just came out of the fryer. You've gotta have one."

"No thanks."

"I know this is tough for you right now," she says, "but preservation is important. You need to eat."

I take a doughnut.

"I have to figure out how to capture this taste on film," Ginny says. "Like in *Willy Wonka* you could just taste everything, couldn't you?"

WE CURVE THROUGH a narrow mountain pass toward the lake my wife and I built our house on. Evergreen trees stand tall along the road, and Ginny has her window down to smell them. It has rained here recently so the air is full of familiar aromas: moss, the smoky taste of damp wood.

"It's so green here," Ginny says. "Why isn't it like this in L.A.?"

"It doesn't rain as much."

"I know that," Ginny says. "But look at all this space. I mean, why can't we just bulldoze some houses in the Valley and get some space back. Plant trees and flowers. Import some interesting African crickets or some lions and tigers. Get a little nature going."

"The San Fernando Valley is a desert," I say. "All the water in it comes from the Colorado River and the Owens Valley. The only things that could live there are snakes and turkey vultures."

"Always the teacher," Ginny says.

I admire her innocence. I do. She doesn't understand what it takes to make life work. She hasn't been taught that animal survival is a miracle. She'll learn.

We're passing familiar landmarks but Ginny doesn't know that, either. It's not her life.

The Branding Iron Café, where my wife and I made love in the men's room. Kenny Rogers was on the jukebox singing about the coward of the county. She'd looked me in the eye and said, "I can feel an egg dropping."

Chance. Natural Selection. Perfecting unknown variables. Drawing Punnet Squares. It came to this.

On the sink, my arm bracing the door so no one could come in, she told me that it would be a girl. We are discovering new places, she said. In my mind I was Louis Leakey. We were restarting history.

"You could talk to me, you know," Ginny says.

"I'm sorry," I say. "I know I'm probably being distant."

"Tell me something, Paul," Ginny says. "Why *did* you want me to come with you?"

This is what we fought about in Klamath Falls, though it was done with different words. This time, I don't think it will end in sex.

"I want you to be a part of this," I say. "To understand what I'm going through, you have to see firsthand."

"Where do you think she is?"

She is my wife. My ex-wife. The mother of my children.

"I don't know," I say.

"Last night you said you loved me," Ginny says. "Is that true, Paul? I mean, is it really true or is it just one of those things people say when they want to end a conversation?"

"We didn't stop talking," I say.

Eleven fingers. It's rare. My research tells me that it occurs in only one-third of one percent of American women. The human hand is a precise instrument. Ginny is a mathematical improbability. Inside her, somewhere, is a strain of corrupted DNA.

"You never stop talking," Ginny says in a coarse voice, but then leans over and kisses my neck. "Pull over. I want you in the woods."

HERE'S THE TRUTH: I don't love Ginny. Her voice sounds too thick to me, like she isn't completely a woman. When she sleeps, I often turn her over and count the vertebrae in her back. I run my finger along her rib cage, feeling the soft grooves that separate her. Her skin gets hot and throbs. I take her pulse and think that she is moving too fast, that her blood must be running backward.

I think I know where she fits in the scale of things.

She is musty with sweat now. Her flesh smells like an animal pelt. It is the dirt in her hair. The wet grass stuck to her cheek.

Ginny is just sitting next to me looking at the map, but I can sense movement inside of her. She is ticking.

"I'm sorry," I say. "I thought I knew where we turned off."

"Don't worry," Ginny says. "Just stop drinking from tin cans. I don't want you completely senile before we're even married."

Our rented Chevy Lumina is parked on the side of the road—a few feet from where Ginny and I had sex. She doesn't call it sex. She calls it "banging." It's a generational thing, she says. I am twelve years older than Ginny. I am old enough to be her brother.

"Let me just get my bearing with this map," Ginny says, "and I'll direct us back out of here."

I know where we are. We are near the place where my wife and I built a house, had children, taught school. It's the place it has always been, but the landscape has changed. This isn't unusual.

At Mungo Lake in Australia, archeologists unearthed four bodies that were twenty-five thousand years old. People had been walking on top of them for years. Picnics had taken place. There were plans to build condos. All the while these people sat underneath the ground, their history being trampled by men in floral-print shirts and women in bikinis.

One day, maybe they will carbon date the condom I threw into the bushes. Maybe they will find traces of children I never had. They will speculate about who I was and how I lived and why I had come to this place, on this date, to have sex with someone I didn't love.

"Okay," Ginny says. "I know where we are."

I TAKE THE Granite Lake exit off the two-lane highway and immediately see the signs for Granite Point Park. When we moved here, Granite Point Park was just two cabins and five or six doublewide trailers. Clyde and Phyllis Duper and their young son Bruce ran it back then as a fishing stop.

Bruce isn't really young. Wasn't really young. He was about our age then.

The signs now proclaim that Granite Point Park is AN IDEAL PLACE FOR A WEDDING OR REUNION. Granite Point Park is WHERE THE WATER MEETS THE SKY!

"You lived here?" Ginny asks.

"Yes."

Bruce's parents, Clyde and Phyllis, must be dead. They were quiet people.

"This is surreal," Ginny says. "I thought places like this only existed in David Lynch movies."

Every thirty yards or so is another sign.

BIGGEST BROWN TROUT IN THE STATE!

IF YOU LIVED HERE, YOU'D BE HOME *BUY* NOW!

FULLY STOCKED WITH LIVE BAIT BITIN' MACKINAW!

"These signs are new," I say.

"They're great advertising flare," Ginny says almost dreamily. "Like old matchbooks. Really wonderful as far as art is concerned, don't you think?"

"I can't really remember what it looked like before," I say. Before Bruce Duper called me on Wednesday to say that he was worried about my wife, that he hadn't seen her in several days and that the house was locked up. Before I drove eighteen hundred miles with a nineteen year-old pierced goddess. Before the roads were paved and the bones were found and the carbon was dated.

She used to say, "You can't race an avalanche."

"Still," Ginny says. "I wonder if your friend Bruce has ever considered renting out space for filming."

How long has it been since I was here last? Three years? A day? Have I ever left?

In 1960, with the advent of potassium-argon dating, anthropologists discovered that the age of the Zinjanthropus site at Olduvai Gorge was more than 1.75 million years older than they thought. It threw off the entire history of the Pleistocene age. Time had to be re-created. Books had to be changed. History had to be adjusted.

It's true: It can happen at any time.

Bruce Duper stands waving on the front steps of what was formerly a small two-bedroom house. It is now a Swiss style chalet. Bruce is tall and husky with a trimmed beard. My wife once said he was a "real man." She once said that he was probably no smarter than the fish he caught, but that he was also the gentlest person she'd ever met. He looks like an animal to me now, all fur and teeth and he's waving his big paw in the air.

I wave back, thinking: Everything here is wrong. I should have never brought Ginny with me. She doesn't fit the scenery. Her body is too lean, her hair too blond. She has eleven fingers and thinks we're in love.

GINNY WALKS DOWN to the marina so that I can talk to Bruce alone.

"Thing of it is," Bruce says in between sips of coffee, "she's always been so regular. She'd come across just about every day to get her mail and such. Pick up some bread and eggs; use the phone if she had to, you know. I got worried when she didn't show for a couple days. Thought she might be sick or something, so I went across with some food and her mail, but she wasn't there. Front door was locked and the boat was still docked."

We're sitting inside Bruce's new house in high-backed leather chairs. He has a view of the lake from every conceivable angle.

"I appreciate you calling me first," I say.

Bruce shakes his head like he's trying to knock out a foul smell. "Paul, we're old friends, right?"

"We've known each other a long time," I say.

"I thought about calling the police straight away," he says, "but I wanted to give you a chance to get up here first. In case, you know, there was something bad out here. I don't think it would be right for you to find out secondhand."

"Bruce," I start to say, but he cuts me off with a wave of his hand.

"I may not be a college teacher in California like yourself," he says, "but I know that family is important. You know what can happen out here, Paul. Things can go fishy for folks when they spend a lot of time out on the water. My mom and dad could tell you stories that would make your skin *run*. Anyway, you're here now. We should probably get the sheriff down."

"Let me look around the house before we go calling the police," I say. "I mean, she could be in Bosnia doing humanitarian relief."

"It's been some days," Bruce says. "You sure you wanna wait any longer?"

"Bruce," I say, "I know my wife."

A phone rings somewhere upstairs, so Bruce excuses himself for a moment.

She's not in Bosnia.

She used to say, "I love people, but I hate gatherings. Isn't that odd?"

People used to make her claustrophobic. She said she could feel them "living" and it made her nervous. We'd be in a restaurant and she'd start counting all of the people.

"There are forty people in here. Forty-two if you count us," she said once. We were eating dinner at a Black Angus in Spokane. "Four of us have been molested or beaten by our parents. Isn't that bizarre?"

She had perfect teeth. Her father was a dentist. Her mother was his hygienist.

"And maybe three or four of us like our sex partners to pee on us," she said.

Her father was short and pudgy. Her mother was short and skinny. She is five nine and weighs 125 pounds.

"One of us has a venereal disease right now," she said.

She's one big living, breathing, recessive trait.

"Sorry," Bruce says, sitting back down. "That was my dad."

So they're not dead.

"How is Clyde?"

"He and mom live in Boca Raton," Bruce says. "He's stopped drinking, which makes everyone a lot happier."

"That's good for them," I say.

"He mostly misses his old boat. Talks about that Fischer like it were a yacht. I keep it clean just in case they pop back in unannounced."

"Have they seen your renovations?"

Bruce laughs and scratches at something on his throat. "No," he says. "I'm trying to make this place over, you know, bring it up to the twenty-first century. Attract a younger crowd. Did you see the signs I put up?"

"Yes."

"I thought it might make this place seem more exciting. What do I know?" We're both laughing now and I'm thinking that Bruce's parents never spent a single day not loving their son. "Listen," Bruce says, serious again. "It's none of my business what you do in your private life, so don't take this the wrong way. But you know how people on the lake are about sex and stuff, so folks are gonna ask me about your friend."

"I don't know anyone here anymore," I say. "Tell them whatever you want."

"How about I say she's your sister?"

There is no one on the lake that could possibly care about me. "That's fine, Bruce."

We stare at each other for a moment in silence. There are two people in this room. If we were the last two humans alive on the planet, what are the odds that one of us would kill the other?

Which one of us has the strongest animal instinct?

Is it the hairy beast with the soft mane of brown facial hair or the anthropologist who can break down each step of the human parade?

"We'll need to rent a boat," I say.

"I already reserved you one down at the marina. No charge on it, Paul," Bruce says. "Mom and Dad consider you guys just about family and would be sick to hear your wife was missing."

"I'm sure she'll turn up," I say. "Probably just a touch of miscommunication on all of our parts."

We both stand up, and when I reach out to shake Bruce's hand, he pulls me into his body and hugs me roughly, slapping my back hard.

He smells like orange peels.

"Hell," he says in a tiny whisper beside my ear.

"It's going to be all right," I say, because I've never been so close to Bruce in my life. I guess I do consider him an old friend, though his parents once told me I was going to rot in hell for trying to debunk the Bible. "Everything is going to be fine," I say, but Bruce is crying and then I'm crying and I can't figure out how long I've been away.

Two

SHE HAS A name. It's Molly. When I hear her name in my head it sounds disembodied. I rarely say it out loud. Couples never do. You only hear your first name when you've done something wrong or when you've done something terribly right.

We are not in love anymore.

I am.

She isn't.

There isn't a date on a calendar that marks the end of us.

There are marks on my chest that do.

Molly and I were married in May 1990. We were both twenty-two; too young, but still older than the woman who wants to be my wife now.

Ginny is leaning over the side of the boat vomiting, lake water spraying into her face.

"Can you slow it down, Paul?" Ginny says in a tearful voice I've heard before. "Can you slow it fucking down!"

"Okay, okay," I say, but she retches again and doesn't hear me. Our rented boat is a rectangular aluminum barge with an Evinrude outboard motor attached to the back. It's for lake fishing and not meant for comfort. My old house is on the north side of the lake, a forty-five-minute ride by boat, a ninety-minute ride by car. The water is rough today from the wind, a cool Alaskan, and foot tall white caps are making the boat bounce.

"Christ," Ginny says. I hand her a Kleenex and she wipes her face. "I didn't realize we were river rafting. Tell me again why we couldn't drive?"

"Remember these details," I say. "It will make your movie seem more real."

Ginny frowns. "Be kind to me, all right?"

I try to always be kind to Ginny. She is a good student. I don't feel compelled to root for her when she takes one of my exams. I grade her as I would any student. Her theories about evolution vacillate wildly, but in an intriguing fashion. She tries to figure out ways that Adam and Eve could have existed alongside primitive man.

"What if Adam and Eve were Australopithecines?" she asked me once. "Couldn't the Bible then just be an allegory about the links in our chain?"

"Could it?" I said.

"Be kind to me," she said then. "Just give me an answer, not another question. My brain is about to implode."

I reach over now and touch her knee. "Are you going to be all right?"

"I shouldn't have eaten all of those doughnuts," Ginny says.

"It's not much longer," I say. "We'll be there before the sun goes down."

"Fine," Ginny says. "There's nothing left inside me now anyway."

AFTER I FIRST noticed her in class, I would see Ginny everywhere I went. She would be the girl checking my groceries at Ralph's, the woman jogging at the gym, the ingenue in the new sitcom.

To make it clear, I'm not a dirty old man. I don't teach school so that I can find women. And I guess it's not really *school*, is it? Community college isn't school as much as it is a way station. No one who wants to be an anthropologist is sitting in one of my classrooms. And, no one teaching anthropology at a community college will ever be an anthropologist. The Leakeys never taught at Los Angeles Pierce College.

But Ginny.

She began showing up during my office hours to chat about *Indiana Jones* movies. She'd ask if I thought they were realistic.

She didn't know the difference between archaeology and anthropology. I explained it to her.

One day she came into my office and asked me if I could drive her home since her car wouldn't start.

"That's crossing a certain line," I said. "The faculty frowns on that sort of thing, I'm afraid."

"I could drop your class," she said.

"Or you could call AAA."

She grinned then and started tapping her extra pinky against her front teeth, like she knew every sweet, evil thing I had in my mind whenever I saw her.

"Tell me something, Ginny," I said. "Do you know why you have an extra finger?"

"It's called polydactyly," she said.

"I know what it's called."

"My mom told me it was because she rubbed her belly so much when she was pregnant with me," Ginny said. "But I stopped believing that after I saw *The Elephant Man* and his mother thought he was deformed because of some elephant accident."

"When was this?"

Ginny paused for a moment and closed her eyes. "Gosh," she said. "I guess that was Tuesday."

We made love that day in the backseat of my Honda.

Made love. That's not right. We've never made love.

Banging.

"What did you guys do for fun out here?" Ginny says now.

"We read," I say. "We talked. Ate home-cooked meals."

"No TV?"

"No," I say.

"I'd be mainlining in a month," Ginny says, almost wistfully. "Not that you could probably score anything out here."

There are a few other boats on the water today, mostly fishermen. In the summer, people from Spokane usually filled the lake with house boats and water skis, but during the fall and winter the permanent residents of Granite Lake numbered under one hundred. Our house is a mile away from the closest neighbor, and now, as I see it rising behind the evergreens, I wish that I still lived in it.

I suppose I could. I suppose if we had lawyers and accountants and screaming fights I could live here year round. I could apply to some doctorate programs. I'd spend two weeks in southern France searching for mandible bones, two weeks at Olduvai Gorge discovering the missing link, and then the rest of the year here, piecing it all together.

"That's the place?" Ginny says, pointing ahead.

"Yes," I say.

"I feel funny about this, Paul," Ginny says, but she pulls out her 35mm camera anyway. "I mean, if she's just sitting in there or something I'm going to feel like a real bitch."

"It's fine," I say, but she's already snapping photos.

It comes to this, finally: Admitting that the worst is possible. Making a decision that you could walk into your home and it could be splattered with blood. You could see your wife dead in a heap, body twisted like they always are in those forensics programs. Your life could disintegrate in front of you and immediately you'd need to figure out how to pick up the pieces.

"The scenery is immense," Ginny says. "Immense colors. Immense smells. It's so large, isn't it, Paul?"

But then it's not you at all. How could it be? How could it be anyone but this person in the boat? This person who just nods while his nineteen year-old girlfriend-fiancée-banger is framing pictures for a movie she will never make; this person who is me.

I TIE OUR boat to the side of the wooden dock Molly and I built during our first summer here. Our old Boston Whaler is tied to the other side and I think about how we had to sell Molly's convertible Volkswagen to buy the damn thing.

"We won't need two cars," Molly had said.

"I don't know anything about boats," I said. "If it breaks down it's not like I can look under the hood and figure out what's what."

"That's why God made paddles," Molly said, and I remember loving her very much then. She was wearing overalls and her hair was tucked under a baseball cap and she kissed me on the forehead to let me know that our discussion was over.

So we gave a Granite Point old-timer named Jersey Simpkins five-thousand dollars for his fifteen-year-old Boston Whaler and figured the rest out as we went along. In time, I learned a lot about boats and about the water.

"How do I get out of this thing?" Ginny says. She's standing up in the middle of the barge.

"You can't be indecisive," I say. "Put one foot on the dock and then step over. If you wait, you run the chance of having the boat drift away a bit and then you're scissored between the two."

"That's great," Ginny says but manages to get herself onto the dock with little problem.

We unload our bags onto the dock and then I just stare at my house. Ginny, even though she's only nineteen, has sense enough not to talk to me for a moment.

Molly and I paid seventy-five thousand dollars for this two bedroom log-cabin.

I know she's not inside.

We bought paintings and built bookshelves.

I know everything about her is inside.

We made love, children, plans.

I know that wherever she is, she knows I am here.

We fell apart, piece by piece, bone by bone, until all that was left were the words, the pictures, and the hope that someday it would be recovered. Someday they would build condos here and everything would be found and put back together in its proper place.

"Do you want to check the boat first?" Ginny says. Her voice is low and sweet and completely female. I look at her and she looks like a baby. Everything is so grand around her. An entire world is standing beside Ginny and she appears so frail.

It's natural selection, I think. The wolves will devour her.

"No," I say and we head toward the house.

THE FRONT DOOR is locked.

"Should we knock?" Ginny asks. She is nervous, I can tell.

"I have keys," I say.

"But what if she's asleep or has a guy over or something," Ginny says. "It would be rude to just rush in on her."

"This isn't a dorm," I say. "This is my house." My voice sounds bitter and raw. Ginny shrinks back from me.

I fumble with my keychain for a moment, making enough noise that if Molly were inside she'd hear it. I put my key into the deadbolt and try to turn it.

"Shit," I say. "She changed the locks."

"Let's just go," Ginny says. "We could drive up to Seattle and get a big room in a hotel and drink coffee and go to that Pike Place Market they always show on TV."

"Wait here," I say. "I'm going to go around back."

"This is stupid," Ginny says, but I'm not paying attention. When could she have changed the locks? At what point did she think that the idea of me with a set of keys to my house, *my house*, was a bad one?

We never even locked the doors.

I walk past our garden, where Molly and I planted radishes and onions and carrots that never grew. There are foot-tall weeds where our small crops used to live and die. I try to peek in through one of the side windows, but the blinds are down.

What locksmith would be willing to boat out across the lake to change two stupid locks? Or drive for three hours?

I reach the back of the house and look around at the mud. There are footprints here in the soft earth, as there always were. We never used the front door. We'd walk out through the back door to where our grill was, or to take a walk among the evergreens, or to lie on the moist ground to watch the stars.

I lean over and trace the outline of Molly's bare right foot.

Mary Leakey found footprints in the lava deposits of Laetoli that were 3.5 million years old. The prints told stories about how our ancestors lived, how tall they were. They detailed the possible start of the nuclear family.

I detail Molly's longitudal arch.

I run my index finger over her transverse arch.

Her prints lead away from the house. They lead to the house. They circle small areas.

There are other prints that run the length of the yard. Some are beside Molly's. Some are apart from the house, running the perimeter.

I stand up and try the back door. It opens into a blackened room.

"Molly?"

Nothing.

"Molly?" I say again. "Are you in here? It's me."

I'm home.

"It's Paul," I say. "Are you here?"

I flip a switch beside the door and the overhead light in the kitchen flickers on.

There are dishes in the sink: three plates, silverware, glasses. The teakettle we registered for is on the stovetop.

Dead flowers are on the kitchen table in a vase we got on our first anniversary.

A full garbage can.

"Paul?" It's Ginny.

"Come around back," I holler. "The door's unlocked."

You prepare all your life to be disappointed by things. You imagine what it will be like to bury your dog, your parents, your children. You imagine scenarios where these things sort themselves out.

"Ugh," Ginny says from behind me. "Do you smell that?"

I don't say anything.

"That's septic," she says.

Scenarios.

In the summer, the septic tank always backed up. In the fall, it occasionally leaked into the soil beneath the house and I'd have to flood the dirt with water until it diluted the smell. Molly used to chop limes up and scatter them around the base of the house.

"I can fix it," I say.

"I hope so," Ginny says.

WE DUMP OUR bags in the guest room.

"I wouldn't feel comfortable sleeping in her bed," Ginny says.

"That's fine," I say.

"I'd feel like Goldilocks," Ginny says and then gives my arm a tug. "Laugh, Paul. I said something funny."

I move in to kiss Ginny on the lips, to show her that I'm alive and well and living in my skin, but she puts a hand on my chest to stop me.

"No kisses until I brush my teeth," she says. "You don't want to taste the Krispy Kreme in reverse like I did."

Here's the truth: She reminds me of Molly. Seeing her here in the house, standing in what used to be my office but what is now a guest room, I want to hug her and kiss her and plan the future. I want to get out the wedding video and laugh at my best man's speech. I want to un-bury everything I kept hidden from her, dust off the age and say, Look, everything is different now.

I want to remove the slashes from my chest.

I would offer her all of these things if Ginny were really Molly.

And that is also the truth.

WHILE GINNY SHOWERS, I go from room to room looking for anything. Molly could be anywhere. There is no crime in leaving your home unannounced.

I start in her bedroom. Our bedroom.

The room she sleeps in.

The bed is unmade, the light summer comforter rumpled at the foot of the bed. Molly's four down pillows are splayed out across the floor, her two cotton-filled pillows, usually placed behind the down ones to be used solely for sleeping, are in the center of the bed.

The napping pillows, always kept under the bed and away from sight, jut from beneath the bed skirt.

On the dresser is our wedding picture.

Molly wore a long white dress and held a bouquet of red roses.

My hair was longer and I was a little drunk.

Looking at the photo, I have to remember these details about myself because I've been sliced away. It's just Molly and her flowers. She looks radiant.

I pick up the picture and hold it against my chest. I want Ginny to walk out and see me and think that this is just terrible, to think that I am fragile and hurting and that only she can pull me through.

But that's not really it at all. I know Ginny won't walk out. She's mid-verse in her favorite Alanis Morrisette song and I can hear the water running. I'm holding the picture against my chest because I am fragile and I do hurt and I miss Molly and wish that I were holding her.

I set the picture down and start pulling out the dresser drawers. They are filled with clothes: socks, underwear, T-shirts.

There's a bottle of Paxil on the nightstand. I touch it and think that perhaps Bruce is right. The lake changes people. The Paxil, however, shouldn't be a surprise. It's an antidepressant.

I go to the closet and open it up. Her sun-dresses are hung up, organized by color, in sharp rows. Her shoes are lined up according to season.

There's a pair of men's boots. I pick them up and hold them in my hands. They are heavy and dirty. The kind of boots a man who liked the outdoors would wear. Stuck in the grooves of the soles are dirt and grass.

So.

You can't be jealous when you have a nineteen-year-old girlfriend.

I set the boots down. There's a large flannel shirt hung up in the closet.

A pair of black socks.

A baseball cap.

I start scratching at my chest.

I don't see any pants.

I sit down on the bed and open up the small chest of drawers on my old side of the room.

They are blue, size 36.

My chest feels hot and I think that everything is fine. No one can live an eternity without feeling loved. It's part of being a primate. It's in our code, our contract with life. I know these things. I teach them. I tell my students that in today's society we don't *need* bonding, we don't *need* to feel guilty for being jealous or promiscuous, we don't *need* to be worried about finding a mate.

We don't *need* anything anymore.

But we want it. Our bodies demand it. Our psyches will bend and twist until it is delivered. It is our contract as primates. We must *have it.*

So I'm fine with this. Molly can love whomever she wants.

I'm beginning to feel a little faint.

"Paul?"

I'm fine, Molly, I really am.

"Paul?"

I just need to sit down and sort this out.

"Paul?" Ginny says. "My god, you're bleeding."

My chest just itches, that's all.

"God," Ginny says. "You're ripping your chest open again. Lie down. God."

I'm fine. I really am.

GINNY FINDS THE iodine in the kitchen. We always kept it in the kitchen in case one of us cut ourselves.

"Why do you do this?" Ginny says. She's swabbing my chest with a cotton ball.

"I don't know," I say.

Ginny stops swabbing and puts her hand against my cheek. "Paul," she says, "there is never a reason to harm yourself. You know that, don't you?"

"Yes," I say.

"I don't want you to feel like you need to keep things hidden from me," Ginny says. "I can handle whatever scars you might have. I'm a big girl."

I know that right now is a time when I am supposed to tell Ginny that I love her.

"It started a long time ago," I say.

Ginny nods her head and starts swabbing my chest again in silence.

I want to tell Ginny that we are capable of great cruelty to ourselves and others. In some cultures, gang rape is considered a legitimate way to punish lazy people. Orangutans routinely rape one another.

So a little scratching is no big deal. In the scope of human development, I'm just an aberration.

"When I'm upset," Ginny says, "I like to go to the mall. That way, I know that I'm still alive. You know what I mean? If I walk through a mall when I'm pissed off about something, I see hundreds of other people. And I just start adding up what's wrong with me and then multiply it by the amount of other people who are probably doing the exact same thing as me. It gives me perspective. It makes me feel like my problems are a lot less significant than I thought they were."

I don't say anything.

"Next time you want to hurt yourself," Ginny says in between swabs of iodine on my torn skin, "you tell me and we'll go to the mall and sort it all out. Okay?"

"I love you," I say, because that's what I know I'm supposed to say. Ginny kisses me once lightly on the chest.

"It's nice you say that," Ginny says, like she knows me better than I could have ever imagined.

Ginny finds some noodles in the pantry and starts boiling water for pasta while I continue looking through the house. I don't know what I'm hoping to find anymore, because I think I've already found enough. Maybe Bruce Duper knew all along and just wanted me to find out for myself.

Molly has gone off with some man.

In the medicine cabinet in the master bathroom I find a prescription for Xanax, an anti-depressant like the Paxil I found in the bedroom. Both are from a doctor's office in Spokane.

Here's the truth: Molly isn't stable. I suppose there is a cause and effect to every illness, and for Molly maybe it was her husband. I've never really been sure. She wasn't, isn't, crazy. It came in waves over her, avalanches she called them, and for days she would be swallowed alive.

It would begin with a migraine that Molly said felt like there were tens of thousands of tiny people pounding on her head with claw hammers. She tried meditation, biofeedback, acupuncture, but nothing could stop the pounding. Then, when the migraine would finally begin to ebb she would sink into this depressive hole.

That's when the madness would begin; the marathon painting sessions, the pacing, the absence of clarity.

Molly would mutter under her breath while stalking from one end of our property to the next.

I told her that throughout human history we have been plagued by man-made disease. I told her that by being this close to uncluttered nature, she would eventually lose this disorder and become closer to her primitive self.

"I'll start living in the fucking trees?" Molly said, hysterical. "You mean to tell me that I'll start living in the fucking trees, you bastard? Is that why you wanted to live out here, so that you could turn me into a fucking monkey?"

"The pasta's getting cold," Ginny shouts.

"So what do you think?" Ginny says.

"It's very good," I say. The pasta is terrible.

We're sitting at the kitchen table, the one Molly bought at a garage sale in Granite City, finishing our dinner. The sun has fallen and already the house is getting chilly.

"I want to take some pictures tomorrow before we go back," Ginny says. "I've got a great idea for a *Dawson's Creek*–style teen drama that would take place on a lake like this. It just seems like it would be an emotional haven."

"We're not going back tomorrow," I say.

"Paul," Ginny says, "I don't mean to point out the obvious, but your ex has just gone off with some guy. I know you don't want to think about it like that, but really, take a reality pill."

"She left her prescription medication here," I say. "Molly didn't like to go to the grocery store, much less on some passion cruise, without her Xanax."

Ginny shakes her head and starts clearing the dishes in silence. After a while she says, "I think you need to understand something. I'm here, and I'm alive, and, you know, I'm the present for you. Not Molly. I came with you because I was worried. Now it's just starting to feel weird."

"I can take you back across the lake tomorrow," I say. "If that's what you want to do, fine. Bruce can get someone to bring you a rental car and you can drive home. I'll pay for it and everything."

"You're not getting it," Ginny says.

I get it.

"There were footprints all over the backyard," I say. "Anything could have happened. She could have been abducted for all we know."

"By what?" Ginny says. "By what, Paul? A Yeti? A Bigfoot? Did one of those 'live bait bitin' mackinaw' climb out of the water and swallow her whole?"

"This isn't funny to me," I say. My chest is burning.

"It's not funny to me either," Ginny says.

I stand up and walk over to the sink where she's scrubbing the dishes and wrap my arms around her. "Two days," I say. "Just give me two days to find what I can find and then I promise we'll leave."

Ginny turns around and faces me.

Small blond hairs grow above her lip and along her jaw line. Her eyes are almond shaped and brown. There are freckles on her nose that turn red when she's angry.

She puts her hands on my face, opens her mouth to say something, and I feel her eleventh finger, that last glimpse of animal that lurks inside her, that breathing, panting beast that I heard after we had sex—banged—on the side of the road.

It is all I can do not to run screaming into the woods.

"This is wrong," Ginny says. "You know it, I know it, and Molly probably knows it. If she comes back here and finds us nesting in her home you're going to have restraining orders and mug shots."

We spend the rest of the night sitting by the fire drinking tea and eating crackers. I watch Ginny in the half-light nibbling on a Ritz and I think that what I have found here is a substitute. Give a starving heroin addict the choice of a pizza or a vial of black tar, he'll take the tar, anything to quell the addiction. We humans are precise animals: our receptors for pleasure and pain are inexorably linked, their borders microscopic—causing us to ask for any stimuli possible in the absence of nothing at all—and so, as I watch Ginny and as I smile and nod at her and as I listen to her hum some nameless song, I think about her here in this house. I think about the sacrifices she has made to please me. And I arrive, finally, at something solid in mind: Being together can be worse than being by yourself.

THREE

I WAKE UP in the pitch dark and hear a man speaking. It sounds like he's preaching. His voice is low and excited and I think that we must have left the TV on.

"What are you doing?" Ginny says, sitting up abruptly.

There's no TV in the house.

"Don't you hear that?"

"All I hear is you shouting about angels," Ginny says. "Are you okay?"

"I'm sorry," I say. "I must have been talking in my sleep."

Ginny pats my leg. "Go back to sleep," she says, "it was just a nightmare."

"Right. I'll go back to sleep."

Ginny lies back down and is snoring from her mouth again in a matter of moments.

Molly claimed I constantly spoke in my sleep. "You curl up beside me and say the most loving things," she'd say. "You tell me how much you love me, except that you don't just say that. Sometimes you tell me that I smell like Christmas. Other times you say that when you were a little boy you dreamed of a person who would save you, and that it finally happened."

"Inconceivable," I'd say.

"Believe what you want, little boy," Molly would say, and then she'd kiss me on the eyes. "But I know what happens when you're dreaming, and one night I'm going to tape record it to use against you."

When I'm sure Ginny is fast asleep, I get out of bed, slip on a sweatshirt, and walk outside. The air is frigid. We're only a few days away from the first good frost of the season. I look up and the sky seems low—like the stars are within reach.

I breathe in deeply and the scratches on my chest open enough to hurt. It's a weakness, this scratching. I know all the reasons people abuse themselves. I know that women are more prone to slash at themselves with razors, eat their hair, chew on their skin. I also know that I am part of the small percentage of men who must hurt themselves to control their anxiety. There are drugs that could help me, that would lengthen this ledge I walk on, that would help me remember what's been lost. Precious Ginny, she never says a word. Precious Ginny.

I walk down to the dock and stand on the first wooden slat. The Boston Whaler bobs in the water ahead of me and I think that it would be foolish not to look inside the old girl.

I'm in here, Paul.

Of course she's not inside the boat.

"You're not inside the boat, Molly," I say. My voice sounds level. Like I'm teaching class.

The lake is quiet tonight and as I walk along the dock

toward the boat I wonder what it was like a thousand years ago. A million. Thirty million.

When did this lake become a lake? Did crossoptergians make the transition from fish to amphibian where I am standing? When the Mesozoic era ended, did the reptiles slither along the base of my house, searching for anything to sustain them? Did they leave their eggs—those tiny embryos that look like our own children—in my garden?

What about a week ago?

Did Molly stand here and kiss her new lover?

Did she run her palm across her soft belly and think about our child, about the eggs that grew inside her, expanded, moved, kicked, and finally found themselves real?

Two days ago?

Did her head fill with pain and suffering, so that she wished she could just unscrew it and toss it into the lake, back with the fish and the reptiles and the moss and the amoebas and the hydrogen and the oxygen and just start all over?

I have a friend at the community college, an astronomy teacher. He frequently corners me to tell me that at any moment the Big Bang could reverse itself. He tells me that the universe could be, at this very moment, going into a reflexive shock wave that would turn the galaxy inside out. He says that all creation would be erased, everything that has ever happened would have to back up again in precisely the right order for any of this—this being human kind, planets, moons, everything—to have a chance of occurring again.

So at this place, at this point in time, anything could be happening. I could be a breath away from the end of the universe. I could be a second away from being a stain on the face of human evolution. My chemicals could be a millisecond away from mixing with a zillion other chemicals as the Earth was imploded and forced to begin anew.

I take a deep breath and wait.

It's foolish to think I can change anything.

I climb into the Whaler and sit down in the driver's seat. It is cold and covered in dew, but I sink into the familiar curves without hesitation. The key is in the ignition still, not a good sign or a bad one. We always left the key in the ignition. I turn it and watch the indicator lights flash on, alive.

The gas tank is full.

The radio cackles static.

I crank the key farther and the engine turns over, wispy gray exhaust coughing from the rear of the boat.

Molly and I used to take the Whaler across the lake to fish in the bass bog near Morgan's Landing on the east side of the lake. I would spend the afternoon casting into the weeds and swearing while she sat with a hat on reading a book. On a good day, I would catch nothing. On a bad day, the Whaler wouldn't turn back over when we wanted to leave and we would be forced to row our small dinghy into Morgan's Landing in search of help.

Now, the boat hums easily, the engine vibrating softly behind me. I walk back and look at it. There's been a powerful new Johnson installed, its rotors clean and unscratched. It's an expensive model, I think, not the kind you can find in Granite City. This looks like something you'd buy in Spokane or Seattle. Powerful and lean, it has none of the rough edges of our old rusted Evinrude.

I close my eyes and there's Molly telling me that she doesn't want to argue about a boat. When did that happen? Years ago, I think. Yes. It must have been years ago.

I sit back in the driver's seat and turn off the engine. I keep the radio on and begin to toy with it, listening for voices. For a while I just follow the waves of static, examining the ebb and flow of the sound, the crashing billows of nothing.

I pick up the handset. I want to say something. I want to broadcast to the world of nothing on the radio a powerful version of my thoughts. I want to empty out my head into the wasteland and let the nobodies listening sort it out.

But all that comes out is:

"Molly?"

"Molly, can you hear me?"

"I'm sorry about all of this."

"Molly?"

"Will you forgive me, Molly?"

"Will you forgive me, Molly?"

"Can you hear me?"

THE CHIRPING OF birds wakes me. I've been asleep in the driver's seat of the Whaler for hours. Sunlight filters through a thicket of clouds and makes the lake look glassy and shallow.

I climb out of the Whaler and walk back up the dock toward the house.

There are footprints leading from the dock toward the house. They run right next to the ones I left on my way down.

I sprint towards the front, shouting her name. I don't want her to see Ginny. We'll never work this out if she sees Ginny.

The front door slams open before I can reach it and Ginny stands there in a T-shirt and shorts.

"I'm sorry," I say. "Is she mad?"

Ginny stares at me, mouth ajar an inch.

"I would have warned you," I say, "but I didn't hear her."

I try to walk past Ginny but she puts a hand on my chest to stop me.

"Are you still asleep?" she says.

"Of course not," I say. "Is she okay? Is she hurt in some way?"

"Paul," Ginny says softly, "Molly isn't here. You're dreaming, or hallucinating. I don't know which."

I turn back and look at the prints in the sand. There is another set leading from the house to the dock as well. I look down at Ginny's feet and see that they are speckled with sand.

"I don't know what to say."

"I came out to see where the hell you were," Ginny says. "I was worried."

"Don't be," I say. "I just got restless during the night. I came out here to collect my thoughts and I just fell asleep."

"You were talking when I got out to the boat," Ginny says. "And you left the radio on."

"I'm sure I was just dreaming."

"You were saying my name." It was cute." Ginny lets me into the house and I can smell eggs and bacon cooking.

"That smells good," I say.

"You must be hungry," Ginny says, "I know you hated the dinner I made."

I grin. Ginny is smarter than I give her credit for.

"The bacon was in the freezer," she goes on. "I hope it's still good."

"I'm sure it will be fine," I say.

"I'm not used to being domesticated," Ginny says. "It's good practice, though."

Ginny goes into the kitchen to finish making breakfast, so I sit down on the couch and try to rearrange my thoughts. Of course those footprints weren't Molly's. What was I thinking—that she had just materialized from the water?

I know about how people die and about how people are born and about the scars they leave. I know how it feels when someone is gone completely.

Like our child.

I remember waking up the next day and having that vacuum sensation in my stomach. I remember thinking that all of my organs had been carted off and that my trunk was an empty hull, like a boat under construction.

We both wanted her. That was never an issue. We both wanted to be parents. We both knew that raising a child was a contract that could not be broken.

No one tested us to see if we were fit to be parents. But who would have thought otherwise? A young anthropologist and his wife the artist. Both educated beyond normal human need. If any two people deserved to be parents, it would be them.

Them.

I can't talk about Molly and me like we are other people. The truth, the real, bare truth is that we were no different from any other twenty-something parents: We drank, we smoked, we lied, we cheated, we fought until it seemed pointless and we fucked like tomorrow was guaranteed. If it had come down to us taking a test to become parents, we would have crammed, stuck crib notes under our watch-bands and taken No-Doz to stay awake the night before the big exam.

Before Molly and I ever seriously tried to get pregnant, I told her what I'd been taught in one of my human development courses: twenty-five to fifty percent of spontaneous abortions are due to chromosomal rearrangements. I told her that we could go to the doctor's office and he could show us the ultrasound and our baby could look like a wolf or a frog or a blob of eyes and fingers with no human understanding.

It was an overstatement, for sure, but I wanted to prepare her for what could be the worst.

And she said, "Flesh of our flesh, Paul."

She said, "You don't understand. There is art in the most deformed creature. We'll love whatever is inside me."

"Do you want toast with jam or butter?" Ginny says.

"Jam," I say, but what I'm thinking is that love isn't nego-tiable—fungible. You can't just move love from one person to another. You can't replace a dead child with a living one.

"Everything cooks faster up here," Ginny says. She hands me a plate with two fried eggs, several strips of bacon, and a piece of toast. "It just makes me feel like there's a magic to the mountains, you know? Something no film has ever really captured. I guess that boils down to story, huh? I mean, I need to come up with a story that really shows how the wilderness can become romantic and mystical and all those great things. Because, and I think you know what I mean, all these movies that I see that take place in the forest are always about men and killing and stuff. Like *Deliverance*. Who wants to pay to see that?"

"*Deliverance* took place on a river," I say. "And it was a book first."

"You know what I mean. Maybe you could help me write it."

"All I've ever written are scholarly papers. I don't have any idea how to write a movie."

"Who does?" Ginny says. "I mean, everyone learns how in some way, right?"

"I guess so," I say.

"Then it's a deal," she says. "You're helping."

We eat the rest of our breakfast in silence, but I can tell Ginny's wheels are spinning. In the six months we've been together, I've learned that Ginny believes anything is possible. She thinks that she can be whatever she wants to be, that no one can hold her back.

Molly was the same way when we started dating. She thought she could become a famous painter, a revolutionary in watercolors. She imagined that together we would create great works of art. "You'll discover an actual unicorn or a Sphinx and I'll do these fantastic renderings of them," she said once. It was before we moved to the lake. "I'll watch you standing up in front of the world's greatest scholars, discussing the jawbone of the Sphinx, and behind you will be my painting of what I think it actually looked like. Can you see that, Paul?"

"No," I said. "It's absolutely preposterous."

Molly looked angry for a moment and I thought that I had said the wrong thing, had ruined a dream of hers. "Well," she said eventually, "I suppose that does sound a little weird, doesn't it?"

"It sounds certifiable," I said, and Molly, with an embarrassed grin on her face, agreed. Now I wonder if it isn't so hard to imagine Ginny doing the same thing.

"There are some things I need to do today," I say.

"I understand that," Ginny says. "Do you want me to come with you or is this alone time?"

"Alone time," I say. "I still worry something has happened to Molly. I'm going to walk back through the woods and see what I see."

"All right," Ginny says. "Maybe I'll take some pictures and write down some ideas I'm having. Maybe later we can talk about story lines and stuff?"

"If that's what you want," I say.

I PUT ON a pair of heavy jeans and a sweatshirt and stuff my backpack with bandages, water and insect repellent. The woods wind around the lake for almost five miles behind my house and eventually narrow into a point overlooking the water that the locals call Loon Nest. Molly used to love to hike to Loon Nest when she was having creative problems, when her hands couldn't create what she was imagining.

It's cooler today than yesterday and, before I leave, Ginny inspects my clothing and supplies. "I don't want to have to come searching for you," she says. "Are you sure you'll be warm enough?"

"I'll be working up a sweat," I say. "Nothing to worry about. I know the area well."

"If you find something," Ginny says, "I don't know, just, be careful."

"I don't know what I expect," I say. Ginny nods her head like she understands exactly what I'm thinking, like she knows that I'm thinking about the last day of my daughter's life and that words are slipping out of my mind and onto my tongue and nothing seems to fit.

"Come back before dark," she says.

"I will." For a moment I think that there are words I need to say to Ginny before I go off. I want to tell her that I think there is something living inside her, that her eleven fingers barely conceal something beautiful. I want to tell her that she is a precious child and that I'm ruining her for someone else who will love her later in life. I want to tell her to call Bruce Duper on the radio inside the boat and tell him she needs to get off the shoreline and into a hotel and back to Los Angeles.

"Be careful while I'm gone, won't you?"

"I'll be sure not to rile the natives," Ginny says.

FOUR

OUR DAUGHTER IS dead. She has a name and Molly and I used it often. We bought her OshKosh overalls. She did not have a vestigial tail. Her eyes were blue and her hair was sandy blond. She slept on her belly. Her fingers looked like tiny sausages. She adored me. She adored Molly.

We made mistakes.

I am walking along the path Molly and I used to take to Loon Nest. It is a rough path, its only wear courtesy of our feet. The path is lined with droopy hemlocks, their egg-shaped cones littered along the ground, and tall false cedars with their scale-like leaves overlapping like shingles.

Molly used to collect hemlock cones, spreading them across windowsills and along the mantel of our fireplace until it felt like we were living outside.

I stop and pick up a cone and several fallen needles and smell them.

We were a family.

Molly catches up to me in my mind, not that she has been far away since Ginny and I arrived here at my home: We are walking along the path for the first time. Our daughter has not yet been born. It is summer, so the air is hot and sweet. Behind us, the sound of a powerboat roars across the lake, doubtlessly towing a water skier.

"What lives out here?" Molly asked.

"Birds mostly," I said. "In the winter we might see some deer coming down to forage."

"No bears?"

"Not that I'm aware of," I said.

"Anything that eats humans?" Molly said, grinning.

"Only mosquitoes."

The trail was tough to cross, branches jutting out like sabers, and we had to cut away tangles of prickly weeds just to walk.

"If we do this enough," Molly said, breaking off a branch in her way, "we might be able to christen this the 'Molly and Paul's Trail.' Maybe get an Indian scout to help us and then sell souvenirs at our house for the tourists who idolize our trailblazing ways."

"Stick to painting," I said.

After an hour we came to a small clearing and set out a blanket to eat our lunch on. A cluster of incense cedars surrounded us, their branches dotted with sparrows and northern flickers pecking away at ants and bugs.

"Do you think we'll live here forever?" Molly said.

"I doubt it," I said. "I mean, no one lives in one place forever, right?"

"I guess not," Molly said. "But, if we have a baby and then we school her…"

"Him."

"If we school *her*," Molly said, pretending she had not heard me, "and, you know, she becomes acclimated to life out here, it would be terrible for us to take her to Seattle or San Francisco to live. She'd be a complete wreck."

"Let's not get ahead of ourselves," I said. "You don't even know if you can get pregnant again."

Standing here along the path now, remembering this, I know that many of the mistakes were mine. I never knew what would send Molly into a fit of depression, never could figure out the catalysts.

I set the cone and needles back on the ground and continue walking east toward Loon Nest. Molly was a perfect wife to me, for a time, and I know that my life now, today, is 180 degrees different from the life I had with her.

Living here in Washington was supposed to be good, safe, easy to negotiate. There were never any risks. In Los Angeles, I live day to day, my existence predicated not by natural selection or the change in seasons, but by traffic on the 405, a sale on ground beef at Ralph's, a crew shooting a movie on my street.

I teach my students the framework of physical anthropology. I tell them stories about discoveries in Africa and China. I never tell them that I've dissected my own anthropology trying to discern how I arrived *here*.

I teach about the step-by-step progression of single cell life to plant life to human life but can't figure out how to save my own existence. Can't figure out how to say the right things at the right time to the people I love.

"I don't want you to think that I don't believe we can get pregnant," I said. "I'm just thinking about what the doctor said."

"I know what you meant," Molly said. "And that's fine. Really." Molly leaned back and closed her eyes. I thought she was about to cry. "Tell me about how we'll teach the kids about God."

"Well," I said, "we'll start by saying that some people believe that we were put here for a purpose and that we were given certain gifts to attain that purpose."

"That's too complex," Molly said, her eyes still closed. "They'll just be kids, Paul."

"Okay," I said. "What if I say that Mommy's parents believe there is a mean old man who lives in the sky who is going to banish us all to Hell for heresy?"

"Better," Molly said, and though a smile cracked her lips, I knew she was still thinking about what I had said earlier. Still thinking that I thought her body would reject me again.

We'd been trying to get pregnant for months.

We'd been listening to doctors tell us that my sperm was being killed by Molly, that they were being intercepted and slaughtered.

There were problems. One doctor said there was something wrong with me.

"Deep seated," the doctor said.

We'd seen so many doctors that they started to melt into each other. Gynecologists, psychologists, obstetricians. I got them confused. There were ones we visited in California, other ones in Washington. I couldn't remember who thought the problem was mine, which thought the problem was Molly's, who thought the problems were ours.

Molly sat up on her elbows and inhaled deeply. "It smells so lovely out here," she said. "We won't ever throw this away, will we? We won't ruin this, will we?"

"I don't know what you mean," I said.

Molly just laughed then, her eyes still closed, her body still propped on her elbows. "It doesn't matter," she said. "This is our home now. This is where we're going to set roots."

My memory is like a flash flood now. I stop walking and look up at the sky, listening for familiar sounds. I listen for the woodpeckers and flickers. I listen for the rustling tenor of the wind that I used to love. But all I hear is the soft buzzing of the few mosquitoes that are still about. They've bumped along the trail with me, searching for one good meal before they find a more temperate location.

We rested in that clearing for another hour, eating our lunch and soaking up our new surroundings. Molly didn't speak much until she got up and began walking the circumference of the clearing.

"Wintergreen," she said.

"Mint," she said.

"Ferns," she said.

"What are you doing?" I asked.

"The plants," she said. "They all have names, you know."

"But how do you know them?"

"I was a Girl Scout just like you were a Boy Scout," she said. "My family liked to camp."

"I didn't know that," I said. "How come you've never mentioned that before?"

"I didn't think you'd find it interesting," she said. "It's not like I can tell if a rock is actually some kind of ancient bone."

"What else do you know?"

"Nothing practical," she said. "I can tie a few knots. I know how to pitch a tent in the dark. Worthless crap, basically."

"That's not worthless," I said.

"It would have been better if they'd taught us how to prepare for manic depression," Molly said, perfectly serious. "Or if they'd held a day long seminar on how to feel if you kept aborting your own children."

The forest thickens and for the first time it's hard for me to see any sky. I'm about a mile from the cabin and I think that whatever I've done in the past hasn't been all my fault. Being with Ginny is wrong, I know that. Morally, ethically, professionally. Ginny has dropped my class but that doesn't stop her from sitting in every Monday, Wednesday, and

Friday. My friend the astronomy teacher thinks that I'm a genius for sleeping with my students. He's older, in his fifties, but he wears his hair in a ponytail and has an earring. He thinks it's hip to date your students because he's been married for thirty years. He says I'm living his fantasy. He says he could never cheat on his wife because he would be consumed with guilt.

I tell him that I'm not cheating on my wife. I tell him that Molly and I are separated. Divorcing. Never getting back together.

"Until the papers are signed and you pay her half your salary," he says, "you are cheating on your wife. In your mind at least, am I right?"

"No," I tell him.

No, I tell him, it's not like that. We have an understanding.

Here's the truth: I can't remember the last time Molly and I saw each other; can't remember how it was I ended up in L.A. and she ended up here. It's like a perpetual stone in my shoe. There are spaces, blocks of time spent with Molly, which feel like they've dissolved, melted into something entirely different.

"The problem I see with you," a doctor once told me, "is that you move things around to suit your own interests. You depersonalize yourself until things seem distorted and unreal. That's dangerous. And it's deep seated."

I WIND THROUGH the trail, stepping over small boulders and shrubs, and through dense pockets of berry bushes. Everything is overgrown. Obviously Molly hasn't been through here in weeks. There would be some kind of evidence: a shoe print, a wrapper from a Power Bar, the label from a bottle of Gatorade.

Molly always littered.

"It's an inherited trait," she'd say, dropping a piece of gum on the ground. "You should know that."

I do know that. But what I never told Molly was that the same reason she littered was the same reason she had a fear of falling, of being left alone, of being in the dark and in enclosed spaces. Molly never wanted to hear my theories on why we act the way we do. She just wanted to keep on living in a fashion she found comfortable. And if that included unfounded fears and littering, then so be it.

Tall weeds sprout up in front of me. I stop and measure one by sight. It's about three feet high. Again, it's clear no one, not even Molly, has been through this area of the trail for weeks. The weeds would be trampled or broken.

"Shit." I lean up against a tree and take a sip from my water bottle. I've been walking for just over two hours and I know that it would be foolish to continue on. She hasn't been through here. The only reason she ever did before was to get away from me or to invigorate her mind for painting. But there wasn't a single easel set up inside the house.

Nobody can say I didn't look for her.

No one can say that I haven't worried about her.

She is my wife and I do love her.

No one can say that I haven't missed her.

Maybe the police are the best solution. She's been gone several days and there's no sign of where she might be. The boat is moored. And she couldn't really have a lover, could she?

The locksmith.

She's sleeping with the locksmith.

"Just shut up with that," I say and a cluster of birds, frightened by my voice, flutter out from the weeds.

She wouldn't take a lover. It's not like her.

No one can tell me that she's in love with someone else.

The police will want to drag the lake. Men in frogman suits will dive off slow-moving boats and search the water for her.

She was probably sleeping with the locksmith all along. How else could she convince him to come out and change her locks?

"Just stop that," I say. "Okay? Finish it. It's not true."

So I'll go see Bruce Duper and tell him that we need to fill out the necessary papers, inform the next of kin (which is me), get a team of detectives out to do some searching because I can't find her. He'll tell me that's what should have been done from the get-go, but I'll ignore him. The guilt can't be mine. Molly is gone because of something beyond my control. If I could have controlled her, we'd be living here, we'd have children playing in the water, fires burning in the hearth, and cones lined up on windowsills.

I CUT THROUGH the underbrush and walk along the jagged shoreline back to the house, weaving into the forest when the water's edge gets sharp and craggy. I find Ginny sitting on the edge of the dock in a swimsuit, a spiral notebook open next to her and her 35mm camera slung around her neck. The day has warmed up to near seventy-five.

"Making progress?"

Ginny whips around, startled. "Jesus," she says. "I thought you'd be gone for a lot longer."

"It became pointless," I say. "No one had walked through there in weeks."

"So what now?"

"I guess have Bruce call the police," I say. "Get a professional out here to take a look around."

"We can't just go running off then," Ginny says.

"Probably not," I say. "I'll have to go back across the lake and call the school, let them know it might be a few days before I can get back. Call it a family emergency."

"Isn't it one?"

"Yes," I say. "I suppose it is."

"I'll have to call my mom," Ginny says. "She'll think I'm dead in a ditch somewhere if she doesn't hear from me."

"She has a lot of faith in me," I say and try to force a chuckle. Ginny's mother thinks I'm a child molester—she's only six years older than I am.

"She just doesn't know you very well," Ginny says. "But that will change."

"Right," I say.

Ginny stands up and wraps her arms around my neck. "I'm sorry you didn't find anything," she says.

"It was a long shot," I say, "but I had to look."

"I spent some time poking through the house, looking for clues or whatever," Ginny says. "I hope you don't mind."

"No," I say. "That's fine. Did you find anything?"

"Your wedding album," she says. "Some letters you wrote. Pictures of your girl."

"We spent a long time here," I say, but inside I'm boiling. *Pictures of my girl.* She had a name.

Your wedding album. It was ours. Not mine. Ours.

"Which letters did you find?" I ask.

"I didn't read them," Ginny says. "There was just a big stack of them tied up with string in a kitchen drawer. I left them there."

"I'll go through them," I say. "Maybe something I wrote Molly set her off or something."

"What do you mean?"

"Molly went through phases," I say. "She'd relive things from the past over and over. It was masochistic, really, but she said it made her feel strong. It was just bullshit."

Ginny lets go of me so that she can pick up her notebook. She starts jotting something down. "That's good," she says. "That's a good character trait. Kind of whimsical, don't you think? I like that."

"It's not a trait," I say.

"You know what I mean," she says and continues writing.

"This isn't some story," I say, grabbing her by the arm. "It's my life, Ginny. Okay? It's my fucking life here. You aren't going to marginalize my wife by saying she had traits. Do you understand me? She didn't walk out of a page. I met her someplace. I met her and we had children and a life and now she's not here. Do you understand me? Am I getting through to you?"

"You're hurting me, Paul."

"Am I getting through to you?"

"Paul," Ginny says too calmly. "Let go of my arm right now. You're scaring me."

I could break her arm. I could snap it like a twig.

I look down at Ginny's arm. My knuckles are white. She's flexing her hand.

"I'm sorry," I say, letting go.

Ginny yanks her arm away and starts rubbing it, never taking her eyes from me. "Don't you ever touch me like that again," she says.

"I don't know where I went," I say. "That was wrong."

"That was abuse," she says. "If there were a phone here I'd call nine-one-one."

"I didn't mean to hurt you," I say. "I just wanted you to stop and understand me. I didn't think I was getting through to you."

"Oh, I hear you loud and clear. I'd hate to tarnish the memory of the woman who left you." Ginny stomps away toward the house, head down like a battering ram.

I know what I'm supposed to do. I'm supposed to call after her, beg apology, whisper into her ear how much I care for her. Make mad passionate love to her in the sand. Like *From Here to Eternity*.

I'll let Ginny dream. She can turn this lousy moment into a movie on her own.

WHILE GINNY SITS fuming in the living room, I go through the stack of letters she unearthed in the kitchen. Most of the letters are recent, from the last year, and when I read my words I feel stupid and small: *I'm sorry . . . I love you . . . I can make it better . . . We can try again.* I sound like a self-help manual—a personal twelve-step program on how to grovel for your marriage.

She never wrote me back, which was fine. I knew her opinions about the subject.

"Are you ready to apologize to me?" Ginny says, standing in the doorway.

"I said I was sorry," I say. "I overreacted."

"You called me a little girl," Ginny says.

"No I didn't," I say.

"You sure did," Ginny says.

I stop and think for a moment, trying to focus on my exact words, but it's impossible. It seems like an eternity ago. "If I did," I say, "I didn't mean to. I know you're not a child."

"I don't really think you do," she says.

"I apologize," I say. "I was just tired and angry and, God, everything just seemed to fall down on me at once there. You can't race an avalanche. I don't know what else I can say."

Ginny stares at her bare feet and wiggles her toes against the wood floor for a long time without speaking. "I need to call my mom," she says flatly.

"I thought we'd do that tomorrow," I say. "Today already seems ruined."

"You need to call the police." Ginny says. "And I don't plan on spending the rest of my life on this fucking lake waiting for you to do it."

"Ginny," I say.

"Either you fire up that boat outside or I start rowing," Ginny says. "It's up to you."

"Look," I say, "if we go into town today, Bruce is going to think this is a great big deal and he'll have people and bloodhounds and all kinds of crap. I don't feel like I can handle that today."

"This *is* a great big deal," Ginny says. "Either you deal with it now or I deal with it. Someone's got to be the adult around here."

WE PILE INTO the Whaler and set off across the lake. It's near three o'clock and the sun has settled low in the sky, giving everything a misty glow. Ginny sits silently beside me, a sun visor tugged down just above her eyes.

The sheriff will have questions for me. He'll want to know how long Molly and I have been apart. He'll want to know why I didn't call him right away. He'll want to remind me that we've met before.

When my daughter died, he came across the lake with the coroner. He sat in my living room and took a statement from Molly and one from me. He said that he'd never had children himself, but that he'd always wanted one.

He told me his wife was dead and that he knew what I must have been feeling.

He looked at me like I was a murderer.

"You're doing a good thing, Paul," Ginny says now, the boat slicing through the water. "You know that, don't you?"

"I do," I say.

Ginny leans over and pats my thigh. "I know you are under terrible pressure," she says, "and that you still have feelings for Molly. You're just not thinking straight, that's all."

"I guess I'm not," I say.

"Listen to me, Paul," she says. "If you start feeling like you can't keep things under control, just tell me. Just give me a sign or something and I'll talk to Bruce or the police or whatever. Okay?"

"I don't know what you mean."

"If you feel like you need to see a doctor or something," Ginny says. "I don't want you to be afraid to be afraid. Do you know what I'm saying?"

"Yes," I say. I know what she thinks. She thinks that I'm losing it.

FIVE

THE MARINA AT Granite Point Park is bustling. We dock the Whaler next to a houseboat loaded with college-age boys. When Ginny steps off the boat they turn and look at her in the obvious way college boys look at everything. Like they are invincible.

"Looks like you have a fan club," I say but Ginny ignores me. She's playing a role now. She's the ADULT. She's the ROCK.

We walk up the landing toward Bruce Duper's house hand in hand. Bruce is standing out front talking to another college kid. This one is shirtless and has a cooler at his feet.

When Bruce spots us, he shakes hands with the kid and meets us before we reach his house. "Damn frat boys," Bruce says, "they bring a bunch of eighteen-year-olds out here to haze them and make them drink warm beer. Every year, one of the kids gets sick and they gotta drag him back to Spokane in an ambulance. You'd think they'd learn."

"You'd think," I say.

"I guess that's not what you wanna talk about though?"

"I think we need to call the police," I say. "There's no trace of Molly out there."

Bruce pinches his bottom lip between his index finger and thumb and nods his head slowly. "Damn," he says finally. "I thought maybe you'd get out there and she'd be sitting on the dock painting or something."

"So did I," I say.

"Sheriff Drew is about all the police we got, you know."

"I know," I say.

Bruce kicks at something with his shoe and then sighs heavily. "All right then," he says. "Let's get on the horn."

"I need to make some calls, too," Ginny says. "Is there somewhere private I can go while you call the police?"

Bruce gives me an odd look. "Everything going all right out there?"

"Yes," I say. "She just needs to call her family. Let them know where she is."

"That right, miss?"

"Yes," Ginny says.

"When we get inside," Bruce says, "I'll show you upstairs. You can call from there."

Ginny doesn't say anything, but I think that maybe she's going to call her parents and tell them that she needs someone to come and get her. She'll tell her parents that they have always been correct—that I am not right for her. But then Ginny gives my hand a squeeze and says, "Unless you want me to stay with you while you make your calls."

"No," I say. "Let your family know what's going on."

Bruce leads us inside and then takes Ginny upstairs. I stand in the entry hall and try to figure out what I'm going to say. *My wife is missing…My ex-wife is missing…My wife, who separated from me after the death of our daughter, is missing.* None of it sounds right. People don't just vanish. There has to be a cause and effect. Asteroid plunges into Earth, the dinosaurs die. Australopithecine moves from the trees and gets stronger and faster, more adept at catching game, arboreal relatives fall prey to natural selection.

Child dismembers animals; child grows up to be a serial murderer.

What had Molly done beside decide that I wasn't a good husband?

Bruce comes down the stairs holding a cat in his arms. "Thought McTavish here might be a calming influence on you," he says, stroking the cat's head. "Saw on *Dateline* how animals help people to recover from all kinds of pain."

"It's a nice thought," I say.

"Hell, Paul," he says, "I don't know what I'm talking about."

"I'm doing okay," I say. "I appreciate the gesture."

"Listen," Bruce says, "I know you and Sheriff Drew didn't exactly see eye to eye when your girl passed. I want you to know that he's a good, honest man. He's got a job to do and he does it. Never lets personalities get in the way. I respect him."

"I know you do," I say. "That's all in the past." Bruce sets the cat down on the ground. When I reach down to pet it, it scurries back upstairs.

"I guess what I'm trying to say here is that I like you, Paul," Bruce goes on. "I think you and Molly are good people. Worked hard on your marriage and it didn't work out. No crime in that, I suppose. At least you took a shot, right? I just don't want to call Sheriff Drew down here unless you're perfectly sure you know what you want to tell him."

"This isn't like when my daughter died," I say.

"Right," Bruce says. "I guess it isn't."

"I understand your concern, Bruce," I say. "But all I know is what you know. Molly is gone."

HERE'S THE TRUTH: I loved my daughter. Every time I looked at her I was amazed by the life we'd created. I'd hold her in my arms and ponder the exact moment she became a human, thinking about the precise genetic code that gave her Molly's eyes and my nose. I imagined the millions of years it took to perfect her, the mutations, the adaptations, the biological changes that allowed for me to hold her in my arms.

She was our last chance. Molly had suffered an ectopic pregnancy a year before our daughter was conceived; a fertilized egg had grown inside her fallopian tube and shredded the duct.

The doctor said, "If it happens again, that's it. There's nothing we can do."

And two years before the ectopic pregnancy, Molly had aborted a child.

We aborted a child.

We'd driven to a small nondescript clinic housed on a tree-lined street in Los Angeles and met with a doctor. His name was Dr. Plinkton. I remember staring at his name badge while he spoke to us, trying to figure out what nationality "Plinkton" belonged to. He ran over our options in a smooth, calm voice.

He said, "Of course you could put this child up for adoption. There are many families who are unable to conceive who would be overjoyed to raise your child."

"That's not an option," I said.

"We're not talking about an option," Molly said to me. "It's a life."

"Not yet," I said. "It's cell division right now."

"I don't know if you two are ready for this step," Dr. Plinkton said.

"We are," Molly said quietly. "We've talked it to death."

It was the only decision that made sense to either of us, no matter how much we fought otherwise. We were young, irresponsible, in debt.

We would have an infinite number of chances to start a family.

Dr. Plinkton handed us a thick packet of documents and instructed us to sit in the waiting room and fill them out. The waiting room was painted a muted cream; a calming color designed to make us feel warm and comfortable amidst seven other women and three other men.

Molly was nearly three months pregnant. We had no insurance to cover the pharmaceutical costs. It would cost us close to one thousand dollars to kill our baby when all was said and done.

"How are we going to afford this?" Molly whispered.

"I'll do whatever I have to do," I said. "I'll sell my car."

"No," she said. "There must be a way for us to put this on credit or something."

I didn't want the people at Visa to know that I was a baby killer.

"I'll find a way," I said and we made an appointment for the following Friday.

We went home and made love that day, out of guilt I think, and partly because we knew we would never make love again without protection. When Molly fell asleep I placed my head on her stomach and listened for anything I could hear. I imagined I could see inside her to our bodiless child, imagined that I could whisper to it and that it could hear me and that it understood that I was sorry.

We made love three times over the next twenty-four hours, and each time I felt an urgency to make Molly feel that I was willing to love her at any cost, that I would always be willing to create life with her, that I loved our baby that was destined to die.

Molly woke me at six o'clock the next morning in a pool of blood. "I'm hemorrhaging," she said. "Oh God."

Dr. Plinkton said, "You could have killed her. Do you know that? You could have killed your wife."

I borrowed money from my friend Vitaly. It cost us $2,317.32 to kill our child and save Molly's life.

Molly spent three days in the hospital with dressings binding her together. She acted cheery, unaffected, even relieved. But there was this shroud of guilt that seeped into her words then, this resolution that she had done wrong, that we had done wrong.

I would leave Molly in her room and walk down to the pediatric ward to see the babies. It was one floor above the emergency room, where Molly was at first, but it could have been another world. There was a sense of equilibrium among the babies, the parents, the doctors and nurses. Nurses hurried between tasks, their voices muted by the thick glass wall separating the babies from the real world. One nurse was patting a baby lightly between the shoulders, another scribbling something onto an observation chart, another still walking with a baby in her arms, gently whispering into its ear. When she got close to the window with the baby, I saw that it was a tiny, shrunken thing no larger than two or three pounds.

"Terrible thing," a woman's voice said. I turned and found a woman with a VOLUNTEER badge on her breast pocket standing beside me. "Mother of that poor child never even went to see a doctor. No prenatal care whatsoever."

"Why's that?"

"You know," she said, "she was just a kid herself. Most of that poor child's bones were broken during delivery; tell you how brittle she is. Her lungs are malformed; eyes and ears probably won't ever work right. It's a shame, isn't it?"

"It is," I said.

"A week in and she still wants to live though," the volunteer said. "Says something about resiliency, doesn't it?" The nurse continued whispering into the baby's ear and walking, as though her actions could possibly make up for all the mistreatment. Like the whispers could somehow change the child's destiny: Blind, deaf, and at best asthmatic.

"Which one is yours?" The volunteer asked.

"None of them," I said.

"Oh," the volunteer said, "is your wife in labor?"

"Yes," I lied.

"Boy or girl?"

"Both," I said. "We're having twins."

"That's just wonderful," she said. "I guess I'll be seeing a lot of you down here in the next few days."

"Yes," I said. "We're going to have quite a family."

Long after the volunteer had left, I stayed and watched the babies. Listened to the families that came to view the newborns, watched new fathers holding their babies like footballs. Babies kept arriving all day, and the families would come and stare at them. There were unlit cigars and back slaps and funny hats. And there were tears, and cries and prayers and sometimes there'd be a grandmother or a grandfather and they'd mutter beneath their breath that something good had to come from this, didn't it? Some babies came swathed in IVs—their arms hooked to hanging interstates of tubes that would keep them alive for a little while at least.

And above me, in a room shared with a woman named Louise who'd had an appendectomy, was Molly, the mother of my abortion.

SIX

"THIS IS SHERIFF Drew."

"Sheriff," I say, "this is Paul Luden."

"Paul Luden?" Sheriff Drew says. "From the lake?"

"Yes sir."

"What can I do for you, Mr. Luden?"

"My wife Molly," I say and it sounds like a foreign language, "is missing. I don't know how long she's been gone."

"Back up here a minute, Paul," the sheriff says. "You aren't still living on the lake, are you?"

"No," I say. "I live in Los Angeles. Molly has been living in the cabin by herself for sometime."

"Are you separated?"

"Yes," I say. "I mean, no, not legally. But we are apart."

"Okay," he says. "Let me get a handle on things here, Paul. When was the last time you talked to your wife?"

"I don't know."

"A year?"

"No," I say. "Within the year."

"When was the last time anyone saw her?"

"Bruce Duper saw her about ten days ago," I say. "He called me after he hadn't seen her for several days."

"Did she normally go days without coming ashore?"

"No." I say. "Bruce says she got her mail daily. He went by the place and said the boat was docked and the house was empty. He got worried."

"All right," Sheriff Drew says. "I'll be there in fifteen min-utes. Don't go anywhere this time."

He remembers me.

HER NAME WAS Katrina. She weighed six pounds and nine ounces at birth. My mother called her the most beautiful girl she'd ever seen. My father said that she smelled like crushed velvet.

Molly just kept crying and calling her a miracle.

Molly's mother bought Katrina a crucifix that hung from a gold chain and demanded that we take pictures of her with it around her neck. "If you make Jesus part of her life early," she said, "she'll always have faith." Molly's mother never met a choking reflex she couldn't exploit.

Molly's father chain smoked Pall Malls and told me that Katrina looked just like his daughter. "She'll grow up to be a heartbreaker, that one."

It was the most perfect day of my life.

I memorized her eyelashes—hopelessly long and curling against the ridge of her orbital bone. I memorized the spiral of hair that circled the crown of her head. I memorized the thick folds of skin under her knees.

After all of the dread, the denial, the fighting—here she was: tangible evidence that Molly and I could make something beautiful. Proof that the chemicals between us were finally in synch.

"She looks like you, Paul," Molly said. Katrina had been wrapped in blankets and placed on Molly's chest. "My dad doesn't know what he's talking about."

"She looks like both of us," I said. "Isn't that how it's supposed to work?"

And that's how it did work. Katrina grew up quickly, it seemed. She was walking upright after nine months, speaking her first words at a year. Her blond hair was long and Molly kept it brushed. She loved to dig outside for bugs — which she then brought to me like an offering. I would tell her what the bugs were, explain to her what their purpose was, how they lived, what they ate. Anything I could think of. If she seemed intrigued by a particular bug, Molly would draw it and then tack it up on Katrina's bedroom wall.

Her name was Katrina Luden and she lived for two years, four months and eleven days. She died on the last day of the hottest summer in Granite City history. She died just like every other child I never had.

SHERIFF DREW PULLS up just as I'm hanging up the phone with my department chair, Dr. Norris. I told him that Molly was missing and that I needed to take a leave of absence, and he just exhaled and said, "This sounds just awful. Any time line?"

"A week. A month. I don't really know."

Dr. Norris paused, and I knew he was trying to figure some way to sound empathetic toward me, a person he barely knew. "Be strong," he said. "And come back when you can."

"I will," I said and hung up, imagining Dr. Norris sitting behind his desk at the college cringing, trying desperately to sound caring when all that is going through his head is how on earth he's going to cover my classes.

Ginny walks downstairs holding Bruce Duper's cat in her arms. Her face is puffy and streaked with tears.

"Are you okay?" I ask.

"They can be just cruel sometimes," Ginny says. "It's like they think I can't handle myself if I'm not within twenty miles of them."

"I'm sorry to hear that," I say.

"My mom wanted you to know that she's sorry this is happening to you," Ginny says. "It was my dad who was being an asshole. He thinks the world spins only for him."

Before I can say anything, Bruce walks in from the kitchen carrying three glasses of water on a tray. "See that Sheriff Drew is here," Bruce says to me and then he notices Ginny. "Maybe it might be best if you had a glass of water and calmed down a bit, miss." Bruce touches Ginny's shoulder lightly, like he's afraid she might be generating electricity, and hands her a glass. "You need anything, Paul?"

"No," I say.

"All right then," Bruce says, "I'll bring him inside and you can get this over with."

After Bruce has walked outside, I get up and watch him from the large picture windows in his living room. He greets Sheriff Drew with a handshake and one of those short "man pats" big men give each other and then the two of them talk with their heads down, like a wind is blowing.

It's not that I don't like Sheriff Drew.

It's not even that I'm scared of Sheriff Drew.

He saw me at my lowest, when my ability to reason was at its worst, and when everything seemed to me to be covered in a haze of hopelessness. What he impressed on me then was that he cared about Molly, cared about me, and started to love my dead child as much as any stranger could.

"He wants to help you," Molly said then. "He wants you to get well."

He did all the right things.

I made mistakes.

HERE'S THE TRUTH as I know it: We do things for people because we are genetically predisposed to it. People help other people because they think it will help them. Applied to our ancestors, altruism was all about genetics: a logical solution of how to preserve the species, cementing the genetic code in our mates, allowing for generations and generations of dominance. In its most animal form, broken down to its weakest link, it was an easy path for the fittest to survive. We've turned it into a form of reciprocal altruism; a genetic agreement that has lasted since we moved from the trees. The nuclear family, it ensures we will survive. But then there are the liars, the cheaters, and the thieves. These people, these animals, would be ostracized from the pack and would eventually die out because no one would befriend them, aid them, and, finally, no one would reproduce with them. Their code would dissolve into the sands of time.

The understated cheaters were the ones who survived everything. They conserved their energy by taking what the rest of the pack had worked for, they reaped the benefits of friendships they did not earn, alliances forged without them. The consequence is that they ended up giving birth to feelings to counter their actions in the other humans: jealousy, spite, indignation.

I think this as Bruce Duper opens his front door and Sheriff Drew ambles in behind him.

"Paul," the sheriff says, shaking my hand. "Shame it's gotta be at a time like this that we run into each other again."

"Yes," I say. "I'm afraid I only see police officers when it's bad news."

"You must be Ginny," the sheriff says, and Ginny nods her head once. "How old are you, ma'am?"

Ginny looks at me as though she wants permission to speak, but I don't move. "I'm nineteen," she says and forces out a half smile. Her hands are clasped on her lap, her eleventh finger barely visible.

"I appreciate you coming out with Mr. Luden," the sheriff says. "It's tough on anyone when something like this happens. You're a nice person for helping your friend out."

"That's kind of you to say, Sheriff," Ginny says.

"Just call me Morris," he says and then turns to Bruce. "Do me a favor, Bruce. Could you take young Ginny outside for a bit so that I can talk to Paul here in private for a few minutes before we get this all started?"

"Sure, Morris," Bruce says. "We'll walk down to the marina and get a couple sodas."

Ginny gives my shoulders a squeeze before she walks out and I think that there are reasons people fall in love over and over again. It's that feeling that someone wants to always help you. That feeling that you're never absolutely alone.

After Bruce and Ginny have left, Sheriff Drew takes a seat at the table across from me and takes off his hat. Then he removes his badge from his shirt and unholsters his gun and places both of them on the table as well.

"I want to talk to you just as two men," he says after a while. "Just Morris and Paul. Is that all right?"

"If that's what you want," I say.

"You and me have some history," Morris says, "and that's fine. I know most everyone on this lake. And you know what, Paul? On the balance, they're some good people. Hell, once in a while someone will get drunk and start a fight or crash their pickup. But I gotta be honest here: it's a good place to live. I think you and your wife are good people. Fine neighbors, I understand. And that Katrina was a treasure, I bet."

"She was," I say.

"You know I never got the chance to have a child," he says. "I think I told you that before. And in the end my wife and I had a lot of hurt about that. Lotta marriages turn sour because of children. For a long time I thought something had died between my wife and me because we were never able to have one—like we'd never have any kind of distinction about our lives. Are you following me here, Paul?"

"I think so," I say.

"I know after you lost your girl things started to go south for you," he says. "I guess what I'm trying to say here, Paul, is that before my wife passed on I figured out that there *was* an importance between us, child or no child."

"I don't think Molly is dead," I say.

"I'm sure you don't," he says. "We're just two men having a conversation here. I just want you to know that I'm not judging you for what might have happened before. Losing your daughter was a tragedy and you're not guilty of any crimes. My hope is that maybe you can reconcile a few things with Molly in your own head, whatever the circumstances are." Sheriff Morris Drew reaches across the table, picks up his gun and badge, and puts them back on. "Now then, Mr. Luden, I want you to think hard: When was the last time you spoke with your wife?"

SEVEN

THE RAZOR OF madness that spread in Molly and me existed before either of us—it existed in the flood plains of the Pongola, along the banks of Lake Victoria on Rusinga Island, and in the woods behind our house on Granite Lake. It settled, though, in both of our minds, at different times and in differing degrees.

For me, it also settled in the folds of my skin, in the lenses of my eyes, and in the fabric of the corpus callosum causing me to live life in this state I find myself now: snagged on a moment of time.

I'm not sure when I began suspecting Molly was crazy. I'm not sure when I began suspecting that I was crazy (though I think it was a long time ago). What I do know is that the two of us lived in some kind of illusion for two years four months and eleven days. We pretended to know what we were doing, pretended to love a child we couldn't define, pretended not to be sickened by the smell of each other's skin.

From where I stand now, it all seems so obvious. What happened to Molly and me during the hottest summer in Granite Lake history didn't happen with words. We'd lost any ability to communicate with each other; our language turned into a series of lost syllables, until all we were left with was a dead little girl.

The truth is lost on me now. I don't know if I have ever known it. But this is what I have said is the truth: Katrina died from hematological malignancies. She was the victim of parents who had suffered "recurrent reproductive losses." In her autopsy, pathologists discovered a tumor in her brain. She could have died in any number of fashions.

It was supposed to end differently. I'd wanted, for a time in my life, to be a medical examiner and forensic anthropologist. Upon graduation from UCLA with degrees in biology and anthropology, I moved directly into graduate programs in medicine and anthropology. I imagined that I would become like the doctors I watched on the Discovery Channel forensics programs. I would sit on TV explaining the crimes of the demented, discerning the variables of human life. My purpose in life would be to solve human frailty.

For two years my days were spent dissecting human bodies and then tracing their very formation. At night, I would spend hours poring over textbooks, drawing distinctions between my medical science and my historical science. Molly and I were already married and she was working two jobs to support my obsessions.

She was so tired all the time. We never had anything.

I made a choice to live then, to make a career out of the human race.

I dropped out of medical school and concentrated on my anthropology, immersing myself in the science of human life, and began helping Molly by waiting tables at Intermezzo in Hollywood. We moved to Granite Lake six months after I finished my master's in Anthropology at UCLA when Spokane City College offered me $38,000 and a chance to improve my résumé by teaching three sections of Introduction to Physical Anthropology. It was going to be a steppingstone to my doctorate. It was only a matter of time before I would be overseeing digs, discovering things, changing history. Molly hoped she could paint well in the wilderness, hoped that for once her mind would be able to slow down enough for her to put brush to canvas.

If Molly had been born a decade later, things might have been different for her. When she was ten years old and started having terrible fits of depression followed by wicked cases of euphoria, Molly's parents chalked it up to adolescence. Now, it has a name and prescription. But that was no one's fault. It was a different time. In the seventies, children weren't bipolar.

To say that Katrina was a miracle is true. She never should have been born. We never should have tried. We were damaged goods—each dead child another scratch on the prison wall.

"A MONTH AGO," I say. "I think I spoke to Molly a month ago."

"Okay," Sheriff Drew says, scribbling on a yellow legal pad, "let me understand something here. You moved to Los Angeles when?"

"A few months after Katrina died," I say.

Sheriff Drew starts flipping through the pages of his pad, looking for something. "Okay, okay, lemme see here," he says. "All right, then, what I have here is that your daughter passed away in September of 1997. Right?"

"Yes."

Sheriff Drew looks up from his notes and stares at me in a way that isn't quite pleasant. A stare that says he wants this moment in his life to end. "That was the one-hundred-years summer, wasn't it? Thought fish were just gonna show up parboiled on the shore it got so damn hot."

"I don't really recall," I say, but a picture opens in my mind and unwinds like an alarm clock: a red sun and Katrina's bleached white body, the clear painful sound of my own voice echoing in the forest. Birds fleeing the trees in a storm of black wings. The gnats darting in front of my eyes. Swarms of mosquitoes.

I sit there staring at Sheriff Drew, my mind shivering with pictures from nearly three years ago, and I wonder if he can see it. If he can look into my eyes and see that there is a vacancy to me. But then he was there, too. Maybe Sheriff Drew understands that time can be like a buried tomb, that what's preserved can be made wretched by memory, can crumble and change.

"Has your relationship with Molly been amiable?" the sheriff asks, staring at his notepad again. "I mean since the separation, of course."

"Sometimes," I say. "She wasn't stable, I'm afraid. After Katrina died and I left, I don't think we were ever all that pleasant to each other. Not mean, you know, but toxic. No good for each other, I guess. But when she was taking her medication it was better."

"What was she on?"

"Xanax, Valium," I say. "Whatever she could get to calm her down. It just depended."

"What about you?"

"No," I say. "Not anymore. I'm fine."

"You have a doctor in Los Angeles?"

Dr. Plinkton, I almost say, but catch myself.

"Not anymore," I say. "I'm cleared to play ball." Sheriff Drew forces a smile out and I realize that I'm being inappropriate, that my words are being scrutinized. "I'm really doing much better."

"Do you know who Molly's doctor in town was?"

"She used to see Dr. Barer, but he retired just before I moved, so whoever took his patients, I would think."

Sheriff Drew rubs at something on his neck and then exhales sluggishly, like he's never been more tired. "Paul," he says after a while, "I'm getting old, so take me through this in a slow fashion: You say you spoke to your wife about a month ago, right?"

"Yes," I say.

"And Bruce Duper told me outside that he and Molly spoke a little over ten days ago when she came in to get her mail. He mention that to you?"

"He told me she came across every day or so for her mail," I say. "So that seems likely."

"Then explain this to me, Paul," he says. "How come Molly told Bruce that she'd gotten into a fight with you just a few days before she went missing?"

"I don't know what she could be talking about," I say. "She doesn't even have a phone out there anymore."

"No?"

"Just the radio on the boat," I say. "When I wanted to reach her I'd either write her a letter or call Bruce and have him get a message to her. She'd either call me from Bruce's or she'd write me a letter. And I can guarantee that Bruce was never privy to our arguments."

"But you just said that, when you needed to contact her, you went through Bruce," Sheriff Drew says. "Might he get a little from both ends? It certainly is possible that Bruce and Molly might have had a discussion or two, isn't it?"

"Why don't you ask Bruce," I say.

"I will." Sheriff Drew makes a note on his pad and then takes a sip of water and holds it in his mouth while he thinks. "How often do you need to contact Molly?"

"I don't know," I say. "We're still married, legally, so there are issues."

"Would you say you wrote her once a month?" Sheriff Drew asks.

"Sometimes," I say.

"And you haven't come to visit during the recent past?"

"No," I say. "I'm teaching again and am involved with Ginny. My life has moved on."

"You've never just shown up then," Sheriff Drew says. "Never dropped in on Molly by surprise?"

"I live a very ordered life, Sheriff," I say. "I don't have room for surprises anymore."

"Do you have anyone who can vouch for you whereabouts for the last few weeks?"

"Maybe," I say. "If I had to."

"Paul," he says, "you're making this difficult on me. You're not on the stand here. We're just having a conversation. I'm trying to figure out Molly's standing, mentally or whatever, at the point Bruce last saw her."

"We're not having a conversation anymore," I say. "You've got your badge on and you have a gun on your belt. This is an interrogation, and I don't see where it's going. I'm here as a courtesy to you and I'm being made to feel like a suspect. And I don't like it, Morris."

Sheriff Drew sets down his pen and glances at me for a long time without saying anything. He may be getting older, but there is nothing slow in Sheriff Drew. His small-town-bumpkin act is not working on me. "Let me tell you something, Mr. Luden," he says finally. His voice is firm and low and I think he has been silent for so long because he did not want to scream at me. "I don't think you coming here is a *courtesy* to anybody. It's your goddamn wife that's missing out there and you're sitting here with some little nineteen-year-old girl pretending to be Mr. Scholar and Gentleman and I don't believe one red cent of it. So let's just get everything square here, Mr. Luden. I'm here to do my job and my job is to suspect people. I'm not afraid to say that your actions strike me as a touch peculiar. If my wife was missing the first thing I would have done was call the police. The last thing I would have done is pile Miss Navel Ring into the car and head up the coast for some R and R while we searched for her. If you want to talk about *courtesy* here, Mr. Luden, it should be that I didn't smack you in the mouth right when I walked through the door."

"I want to talk to a lawyer," I say.

"I think that's a good idea," he says, and then pulls out a slip of paper from his breast pocket and slides it over to me. "That's a search warrant. As a professional *courtesy*, I'll wait for you to call a lawyer before I execute it."

GINNY AND BRUCE return while I'm talking to my lawyer on the phone. "What's going on?" Ginny mouths to me but I put a hand up to quiet her. My lawyer is an old friend from college named Leo who specializes in personal injury cases. He is completely confounded by what is occurring.

"Tell me again exactly what you told this cop," he says, and I repeat our entire conversation. Ginny sits down beside me and listens intently. "Okay," Leo says. "Okay. Nothing incriminating in that."

"I haven't done anything," I say. "There's no crime here."

"Let's just reserve judgment on that sort of thing for now," Leo says. "You have no idea what kind of crimes Barney Fife thinks you *might* have committed, and that's what counts."

"Can you fly up here?"

"Not for another two days," he says. "I'm trying a slip-and-fall against a supermarket that should be wrapping up posthaste. Right now, everything seems in order. You've got nothing to hide, am I right?"

"You are right."

"And if Andy Griffith goes over to the house there's nothing of merit to discover, correct?"

"Nothing of mine."

"Fine," Leo says. "Just fine. If it looks like he wants to arrest you or something, call me on my cell phone and I'll post bond for you. How much equity do you have in that house?"

"I don't know, Leo."

"Fine, fine, no problems," he says. "Call me if anything happens and I'll be there ASAP."

I hang up and Ginny is near tears. "What's happening?" she says.

"The sheriff has a search warrant for the house," I say. "Leo says it's perfectly normal."

"Are you under suspicion for something?"

"No," I say. "The sheriff's just doing his job."

"Then why were you on the phone with Leo?"

I want to tell Ginny that there is a back-story to all of this that she'll never understand no matter how many films she wants to make. I want to tell her that she doesn't have the capacity to understand the dialogue that has transpired. I want to tell her that she does not know a single thing about me. "Just to be safe," I say and before I can say anything else, Bruce Duper walks into the room with two thermoses.

"Filled these up with coffee for you," Bruce says. "Sheriff is out front waiting on you with one of his deputies. Looks like it's gonna be a long night."

"Ginny, maybe you should stay here with Bruce," I say.

"I don't want to do that," she says. "I belong with you."

I look outside and see Morris sitting on the hood of his car with a tall, thin deputy and I think all of this is about gravity. There's no part of me ruled by nature anymore. There is no animal in me that keeps me poised on the face of this earth. What it has all boiled down to, what it has always been, is about getting some gravity beneath me. I frown at Bruce and take the thermoses from him. He looks scared and baffled; like it is his home they are about to search.

"I want you to know that I didn't tell the sheriff anything I didn't tell you," Bruce says.

"There's nothing to be concerned about," I say. "Maybe he can find my wife."

Ginny sucks her breath in and I think that it doesn't matter how much air she breathes, how much love she gives me, how many times we *bang*, it all comes down to the fog in my mind and the trouble within Molly's.

"Paul," Bruce says, "this is all going to turn out fine."

"You're right," I say because nothing worse can ever happen than losing my little girl. Nothing will ever be as final. "You are absolutely right."

EIGHT

FOR THREE MONTHS the sun bleached everything that washed up in front of our cabin: ducks, fish, candy bar wrappers. Katrina wasn't allowed to leave the house without a hat and sun block.

At night the sunset would turn the sky red and then purple, but the heat would persist. We drove into Spokane and bought oscillating fans to put into every room. Nothing helped. I showered four times a day.

"We should fly to L.A.," Molly said once the heat had persisted for over a week. "Rent an apartment in Santa Monica until the heat breaks."

"What if it never breaks?" I said. "What if this is the beginning of the end and we're all just going to bake to death?"

"Paul," Molly said, "be serious. It can't be healthy for the baby to be in this kind of heat."

"I can't just pick up and leave," I said. "Who will teach the summer session?"

After a month, Molly began to turn.

"Tell me something," she said. "Tell me why we sit here and let the sun beat down on us? Tell me why we don't just kill ourselves now and let the scavengers pick us apart."

She'd stopped taking her medication. She'd stopped bathing Katrina. All she painted, over and over again, were copies of clinical drawings of the female reproductive organs. Eventually she stopped doing even that.

So I took care of Katrina. I bathed her. I read to her. I walked with her. I told her that we loved her so much. I told her that sometimes parents aren't prepared to deal with certain things.

I told her that we'd made some mistakes but that we were going to turn out all right.

After two months, Molly stopped speaking to Katrina altogether; she referred to her as "the child" and "that" and sometimes "her." The truth is that by this time I had begun to see through Molly. I began to deconstruct her. She turned into an abstract principle to me: a vessel for Katrina. At night we would still make love, but it was wordless, algebraic sex. Something we both needed to do to complete whatever equation we were both working out.

For me, the math was simple: I wanted another child, another piece of Molly, another piece of me, another piece of whatever child we'd killed before. It didn't matter that Molly was slipping in and out of herself. It didn't matter that I couldn't figure out how many hours had passed at any given time.

Everything about that time seems liquid and out of focus now. The truth is that I haven't been well since Molly's abortion. The truth is that I began to look at Molly and Katrina as animals, as experiments in human anthropology, as verbs and nouns that lived in my house.

I didn't know all of that then. I didn't know all of that until after Sheriff Drew came across the lake with the coroner
to pick up my girl. I look at Sheriff Drew now, sitting beside
his deputy at the front of the police boat as we cut across the
lake, and wonder what he makes me for. Does he think that
we will get off the boat at our dock and he will find Molly
like he found Katrina?

Into my head floats my first image of Sheriff Drew. I see him
jumping out of a tugboat and storming onto the beach with a
rifle in his hands, screaming like an animal. But that's not right.
That's John Wayne in an old movie my father used to love.

I close my eyes and listen to the water crashing around
the boat. I am vaguely aware that Ginny is saying something
to me, but I'm trying to focus on the day I first met Sheriff
Drew, trying to reason with the visions of him I have, trying
to remember the endings and the beginnings of everything.

It comes to me all at once: A small boat with a medium-
size Evinrude outboard engine. It slides up onto the beach
and Sheriff Drew, wearing a tan short-sleeved shirt with
sweat rings around the neck and arms, jumps out. He shouts
for me to stand still but I'm running into the trees with her
in my arms. She's so light in my arms. She makes me feel like
I'm floating, like I'm above the trees and above the screams
I hear behind me. When I finally stop running I look down
and see that there are scratches on her arms and face from
the branches. I look up and he's standing there with his gun
out telling me to set her down. Behind him is a panting man
wearing glasses, the coroner. He also tells me to set her
down, that they are here to help, that this is all going to be
fine, just fine.

I open my eyes and Ginny is glaring at me.

"Are you listening to me?" she says.

"Everything's going to be fine," I say.

Sheriff Drew turns around at the sound of my voice and
regards me with a slight nod of his head, like he wants to believe me.

"Do you see," Ginny is saying, "the way the mountains look flat in front of us?"

"Yes," I say.

"It's a trick, you know," she says. "Your eyes make them look like walls, like they've been fused together and slapped onto the horizon. Are you getting my point, Paul? About everything I've just said, are you piecing it together?"

"Yes," I say, because all I have heard are memories from three years ago, visions that happened and didn't happen, a past and a present that won't stop colliding, until I'm not sure which is which.

"We're going to get through this, and later it will all seem just like a mirage," Ginny says. "A year from now, Paul, when Molly is fine and we're back in California, you'll be able to look back at this. Right?"

"Yes," I say. Yes, everything is going just as planned. A year from now I'll be married to a human mutation, we'll try to have children just as Molly and I had tried, we'll review charts and graphs that detail my sperm count, we'll hold hands and cry when we get the first look at the ultrasound, and all the while I'll be wondering how many fingers it will have, how many flippers it will have growing from its back, how many different animals it will have floating in its blood.

How long until it dies?

"THIS IS HOW it's going to work," Sheriff Drew says. We're standing on the front porch of the cabin. "Deputy Lyle and I are going to go room to room. This isn't like the movies. We're not going to break anything, we're not going to cut open your couch, we're just looking for anything we might find important. And everything we take will be catalogued. Okay, Paul?"

"That's fine," I say. "Where do you want us?"

"Just sit on the couch," he says. "If we need you, we'll let you know."

I open the cabin door, and it seems different to me; like it has grown larger and emptier since we've been gone. I stand there in the doorway for a moment and it feels like I've been carved in two. Like the person who slept here last night and the person standing here now are completely separate.

"All right then," Sheriff Drew says. "Why don't you two take a seat and let Deputy Lyle and me get to work."

"This is insane," Ginny says after the sheriff has gone into the kitchen and Deputy Lyle has moved toward the bedrooms. "I mean, what's with the hoopla of a warrant? Couldn't they have just as easily asked you if they could search the house?"

"He's just doing his job," I say. "Everything by the book."

"Bruce said he thought the sheriff was a fair man," she says. "That he would give you a fair shake. Why would he say something like that?"

Inside the kitchen, I see Sheriff Drew pick up the stack of letters I've left on the table. I wonder if he'll read each one. I wonder if he'll sit in his sweet little home in Granite City and pore over each sordid detail. I wonder if he'll go to the Branding Iron Café and listen to Hank Williams songs on the jukebox while he reads my pleas for forgiveness.

"The sheriff investigated Katrina's death," I say. "Bruce was probably just thinking out loud."

"Wait a minute," Ginny says. "Wait, wait, wait. You said your daughter died of natural causes. You told me she died out here from some kind of disease. Isn't that what you told me?"

Sheriff Drew unties the string around the letters and starts examining the postmarks.

"Is that what I told you?"

"Yes," she says. "God damn it, Paul. What's going on here?"

"He was just following procedures," I say. "Somebody dies out here, he gets notified. That's just how it works."

Sheriff Drew pulls the first letter out and runs his finger along the edge of it slowly, like a groan, before he unfolds it. I want to run into the kitchen and tell him that he is not allowed into my mind. That he can't have access to my Molly.

"Paul," the Sheriff says without looking up, "I'm gonna have to take these letters. I'll bring them back when this is all taken care of."

"Those are personal in nature," I say.

"They won't be up for display; and at this point I need to consider all of my options. I know you understand," he says and shoves the whole stack into a clear plastic evidence bag and seals it.

Ginny puts her hand on my knee and I hear her say that she's confused, that she doesn't think I've told her the whole story about Katrina dying, about why Molly and I split up.

"There were problems," I say. It feels like there is a dark cloud behind my eyes, like everything is slowing down for the first time. I look past Ginny and see the sheriff. He is watching us. I see him as I did that first time in the clearing: an impostor, a badge, a gun, a hat, words that mean so much to so many but that can do nothing for me. I trace him back through time, through the ages, through the sand and the dust, beneath the footprints and the bones, across the plains and down into the Omo River in Ethiopia, until he is nothing but a single cell. Until he becomes irrelevant.

"Paul," Ginny is saying, but inside I'm running through the trees toward the water with Katrina in my arms. I'm sprinting down the dock and Sheriff Drew is shouting that he'll shoot, Molly is crying and telling me to just stop running, the panting man in the glasses is screaming that she's dead, she's dead, and all I can do is leap into the lake.

My feet sink into the sand, the water spilling over my shoulders, my neck, and my head. My eyes are open and everything is blurred and hazy and I'm floating along the bottom. I hold her in my arms and twist until I am on my back looking up at the ripples in the water, rays of sunlight cutting the surface. We can stay here forever, Katrina. We can stay until the forests have petrified, until the sun has boiled the earth. We can stay until we grow gills and learn to breathe the water.

"He's hyperventilating," I hear Sheriff Drew shout. "Lyle! Get in here!"

We can stay until they've solved every equation, until X and N are determined.

"It's okay," Ginny says.

And then I am ripped from the water, my daughter tumbling from my arms, sinking, slipping farther and farther away.

NINE

IF THE TRUTH were known, I've never wanted to be a person who passes out. I've never wanted to be a person who keeps things inside until he is physically ill. I've never wanted to be anything less than perfect—from my science to my wife to my child to my dreams—I've always wanted to be the ideal.

I am a failure at so many things.

It's five o'clock in the evening and I've been asleep. Ginny is sitting next to me on the bed. I can see Sheriff Drew out in the hallway flipping through his notebook.

"Feel better?" Ginny says.

"How long have I been asleep?"

"About an hour," she says. "Sheriff Drew called a doctor. He's going to be here in about forty-five minutes or so."

"I don't need to see another doctor," I say.

"Paul," she says, "it's not normal to hyperventilate like that. I think you're suffering exhaustion or something."

"That's Hollywood speak for being a drug addict," I say. "Everything just got mottled there for a minute. I'm fine now."

"Well, he's on his way anyway," Ginny says. "You can tell the doctor how you feel."

Sheriff Drew walks into the room holding the men's clothes I found in Molly's room. "How you doing?" he asks.

"I'm all right," I say.

"You wanna tell me what happened there?"

"I just started thinking about worst-case scenarios," I say. "Started thinking about the past. Lost control of my feelings and it got the best of me. I'm not used to that anymore, I guess."

"Ginny tells me you've got some scratches on your chest," he says. "That a related problem?"

"Yes," I say. "Nervous reaction I have. I've had it all my life. I'm genetically predisposed to hold my emotions in. At least that's what my mother always told me."

Sheriff Drew smiles lightly and then shakes his head. "I've heard that about myself before," he says. "But I never took it to your level, I'm afraid."

"Few do," I say, and for a moment the three of us are silent and I think that maybe Sheriff Drew has some odd habits, too. Just like the rest of us.

Eventually the sheriff remembers the clothes in his hands. "These yours?"

"No," I say. "They were in Molly's room when we got here."

"So you touched them?"

"Yes," I say. "I don't think Ginny did, did you?"

"No," she says. "I just left them where they were."

"I can't tell you how much I wished you'd called me earlier," Sheriff Drew says. He's mad now, but trying to keep it buried. Trying to stay calm.

"I'm sorry," I say. "I know you think I'm some kind of monster, some kind of person who doesn't know how to properly care for people, but it's not true. I just thought she'd be here."

"I don't think you're a monster. People can be all sorts of things, but not monsters. You're flesh and blood, Paul, just like the rest of us," he says. His voice is annoyed, like he is talking to a child who has spilled its third straight cup of milk. I know this voice. It used to be mine. "To the best of your knowledge, did Molly have a boyfriend?"

I think about the locksmith, the lover I've convinced myself of, the lover who has no name or face. "Bruce would probably know better than I would," I say. "We never discussed that sort of thing."

"So she doesn't know about Ginny?"

"I guess she does," I say, more for Ginny's benefit than for the truth. The truth is that I can't remember what I told Molly about Ginny. An image floats into my mind of Molly standing in the kitchen asking me if I have anyone, but I don't know if I've dreamt it or not. "I suppose the answer is that I never asked her if she had anybody."

Deputy Lyle walks into the room and takes off his hat, like he hasn't been rifling through my house for the last two hours. "Pardon me, Morris," he says. "But I found some pictures in the other bedroom that I thought you might want to see."

"Molly is a painter," I say, but it comes out sounding defensive.

"I know that, Paul," Sheriff Drew says. "You two stay put. Why don't you get some more rest until the doctor gets here."

"I'm not tired," I say.

"Well, then just sit here," he says. "And don't touch anything else."

MOLLY PAINTED AND drew whatever was on her mind. She would paint the face of her mother over and over again, etching lines into her cheeks, dark circles beneath her eyes, a crooked tooth where none existed.

She'd sit with Katrina and tell her stories about each picture. There was a painting she made after the ectopic of a giant whale floating over the Los Angeles skyline that Katrina always loved. Molly would tell her that the whale was a super hero, a mighty defender of honor and truth for women. Katrina didn't know what Molly was talking about, of course; she just liked to see the enormous whale.

"Why a whale?" I asked Molly after she'd finished telling Katrina a new story about the picture. It was the same summer our girl died. "Why not a bird or a dog or something?"

"Whales are continuous," she said. "No necks, you know. They can wrap themselves into circles. And they're mammals. They're just like us, but without all the unnecessary words."

"I don't understand," I said.

"Without a neck," Molly said, "they're just these great big heads. These heads that live and breathe and procreate. They don't have to worry about anything below anything. All they have is all they have. And their words are music."

"But that's not true," I said.

"It's true for me," she said. She made a humming noise then, like she was processing information. "What do you know about women, anyway?"

"I don't know what you mean."

"I mean, do you think I can't act independently of my organs? Do you think I can ignore my ticking clock? Do you think I don't know that I'm going to spend the next sixteen years of my life raising a child while you go out on digs? Do you think I don't notice that my passion for you isn't the same as it was before Katrina was born?"

"Why are you saying this to me?"

"You need to hear it," she said. "Let's face reality here, Paul. What are the odds of us getting a divorce? Three to one? Two to one? Where do you place them?"

"I don't want to talk like this, Molly," I said.

"Then maybe you should pay attention more often," she said. "I'm not happy anymore. This medication makes me feel like a robot. Katrina wears me out and you don't notice anything but a stupid whale in a painting. Why not ask me why we haven't had a meaningful conversation all summer."

"It's the heat," I said.

"It's you," Molly said.

There are some things I can't erase. There are some things about the last days of my daughter's life that are still clear to me, no matter the angle of the light or the density of the air. And this: I remember Molly got up from the couch and started to walk toward the front door, as though she was going to leave. She stopped, though, her hand on the doorknob, and started laughing. "You know what, Paul," she said, still facing the door, "I know that I'm replaceable to you. I know that after I'm gone there will be someone else who will love you. Is that right, Paul? Do you think that's right?"

"No, you can't ever leave me. You leave me and I'll come with you," I said. I was trying to sound light. "You move out, I'm coming with you."

"You'd just erase me and draw another," she said and went out the front door.

Ginny is not Molly. I know that now. They are different breeds, different branches of the females of our species. What intrigued me about Molly at first was trying to understand why she felt so strongly about me. Here she was: an artist from a wealthy medical family. Here I was: a failed doctor and an aspiring anthropologist who came from a family of aspiring anythings. My mother always wanted to be a lawyer, a doctor, a writer, an actress. She worked for AT&T as an operator for thirty years. My father wanted to be a carpenter, a commercial fisherman, an astronaut. He managed a series of chain restaurants his entire life, culminating in retirement from Marie Callendar's a few years before he died.

In the end, what I found most interesting about Molly was her anthropology. Her beginnings. I started to wonder about what parts of different animals she had inherited. What traits of primitive man were still most prevalent in her? What portion of her brain was still living in the primordial swamp? What had she transferred to my daughter? What had made my child so sick?

What makes me believe that Molly and I were meant for each other is the way she never spoke to me like a patient. Even when she was at her sickest, even when I was at my lowest, she always spoke to me like another human should. There was nothing abstract in her back then.

Now, today, with Ginny on this bed in this house I used to live in, I have come full circle. Sheriff Drew is rummaging through our things, again. A doctor is on his way to see me, again.

I take Ginny's hand and hold it.

"You're shaking," she says.

"This is the worst possible thing," I say.

"Paul," she says, "tell me the truth. Tell me what went wrong here with your daughter."

Ginny speaks in words that she thinks make good dialogue. She doesn't understand that I've been trying to get to the truth since before Katrina died.

"It's not that easy," I say. "You'll leave me if I tell you."

"I'll never leave you," Ginny says. "Don't talk like that." Sometimes, I say things to hear how Ginny will respond. Sometimes, I say things to her that I've said to Molly. Ginny squeezes my hand tightly; her thumb caresses my wrist, bouncing between the vein and the artery that lead directly to and from the heart. "Let's get married when this is all over. We'll just fly to Vegas. We'll do it, Paul. We'll be together forever that way."

"I'm not even divorced," I say. "I've been married. I've had children, you know. I've made mistakes with everything I've ever loved. Why would you want to be with me? You're a young woman, Ginny. I'll disappoint you."

Ginny lets go of my hand and leans back onto the bed with her eyes closed. Her breath is coming out in these tiny rasps, like a sick animal. "I won't let you do this to me," she says quietly. "All I want from you is the truth. Why is that so difficult?"

I lie beside Ginny and curl my arm around her. Outside the wind begins to kick up through the trees and I think now would be the time to take Ginny outside to show her the sunset. We could stand on the shore and watch the ripples of water lap against the sand. I could tell her I love her. I could tell her that I have always loved her and that the truth is very simple. I could tell her that the truth of it all is that I killed my daughter and got away with it.

"I love you," I say.

"Do you?"

"You are precious to me," I say, my voice sounds round near the edges. I am a teacher again. I am explaining the problems with an assignment, but I mean it. "We met at the wrong time, I think. You need someone else." I am a tape recording, repeating words I have memorized. Words I have said in my head a thousand times.

Ginny turns her back to me so that I won't see her crying. I run my hand down her spine, but she sweeps it away. "Don't," she says.

"I'd shed my skin for you," I say. "I want you to know that."

I stare at the wall across from Ginny and try to concentrate on excluding her—on making her just an object in the room. Her breath becomes only a sound, her smell just a scent until I feel like I am in the room alone. Until the only thing I can hear is my own heart beating in my ears, the first sounds Homo sapiens ever got accustomed to.

And then, in the clear of my mind, I see what I suspect Sheriff Drew and Deputy Lyle are looking at: drawings of Katrina. They are drawings of her every organ, her every limb, the tumors in her brain. They are concise outlines of everything that made Katrina real, and I am sorry I ever saw them. I am sorry I ever drew them. I am sorry for making Molly teach me.

And there are autopsy photos of Katrina and drawings of Molly. They are just lines: sketches of life, of death, of the undeterminable consequences of time and suffering.

Here's the truth: I used to feel like the whale in Molly's painting. I used to feel like I was floating over a sea of water that I could never swim in. I felt like every thing was contained in my head. Sometimes, I would go to school and feel like a completely different person. I would stand in front of the classroom retelling human history like I was completely certain that it was true. When class was over, and the room was empty, it would feel like I had played a game of hide-and-seek and I was the only one who wasn't found.

What if I have never been found? What if I am a completely different person from who I once was? Who would know if I didn't? Who could tell me where I have hidden?

"I do love you," I say. "And when this is all over with we will get married. We'll have a huge wedding. We'll invite all of your friends. Maybe we'll go to Hawaii and have it on the beach in front of some magnificent resort. Would you like that, Ginny?"

"Don't say that just to make me happy," she says, her voice just above a whisper.

"I'm not," I say. "When this all over, I'll tell you everything that happened with Katrina. Molly and I will get divorced and we'll make the plans. We'll do it. We'll do whatever you want."

Ginny flips over and faces me. There are streaks of tears covering her face, but she is smiling. "Paul," she says, "I'll make you so happy."

"I know you will," I say.

"And we'll have more kids, Paul. We'll have as many as you want. We'll have to move into a shoe we'll have so many kids!"

"We'll have quite a family," I say.

Ginny wraps her arms around me and squeezes tight, like she's afraid I might get up and run. I bury my head into her and all I can smell is her shampoo and perfume and all I think is that I've had this same conversation before. All I can think is that right now Sheriff Drew is prying through my precious drawings of Katrina. He is staring hard at the charts and graphs I've made about Katrina. Deputy Lyle is trying to make sense of what the hell he's looking at, and I'm holding on to Ginny and we're rocking back and forth and she's whispering into my ear and crying and I'm telling her that I love her. I tell her over and over again that I love her, that I want her, that I need her. I will never be better to her than I am right now. She will look back on this moment with a sense of glory that will never abate. I close my eyes and think about the day Katrina died. I try to think about the truth. I try to think about how I felt at the very moment she stopped breathing.

"Our house will be like a shrine," Ginny is saying. "We'll always have flowers and pictures."

"Are you afraid," I ask, "that there will be nothing left of for us when this is over? Are you afraid of that?"

"Everything is left," she says.

We could both die right here and it would be fine.

"Paul Luden," Sheriff Drew's voice echoes in my head. I keep my eyes closed and pretend not to hear it. Pretend that it isn't bouncing off the walls of my head, between my eyes and out my mouth. "Paul, c'mon now." Ginny has let go of me but I'm still holding on to her. "Let's not make this hard for everyone. Be a gentleman."

"Paul," Ginny says, "let go."

If I keep my eyes closed and hold onto Ginny I can just dream this all away. I can make this all disappear.

"Let go of the girl, Paul," Sheriff Drew says.

I can tell the sheriff that it is all art. That even our earliest ancestors expressed themselves with ritualistic drawings. I can tell him about Lazaret Cave in southern France where each dwelling archaeologists unearthed had a severed wolf's head at what amounts to the front door.

"God damnit, Paul," Sheriff Drew says. "Let's not go through this again. For the sake of Ginny here, just let go and stand up."

For the sake of Ginny.

For the sake of Molly.

For the sake of me.

I have made so many mistakes.

The truth is that I never should have come back. The truth is that I've never left.

"I'm placing you under arrest," Sheriff Drew says and then handcuffs my wrists.

"No," Ginny cries. "You can't just arrest him! He hasn't done a single thing."

"Miss," Sheriff Drew says, "you don't even know half the truth, do you?"

TEN

ABOVE ALL ELSE, I needed someone to save me. There were problems. There are problems. The sheriff says there must be something wrong with me, that there is something inside me that isn't firing right.

Dr. Loomis, that was his name. He was the doctor who told me I had problems and that they were deep seated. He told my parents that I had a dissociative disease, that I rearranged my life according to my own reality, that I depersonalized the world to such an extent that I might do myself harm. "Puberty," he wrote in a report to my parents, "will be a period of great change in Paul. I recommend aggressive medication until that time."

Aggressive medication. Weeks that turned to months that became years under his care and never once did he tell me the truth about myself. I had to find it in a file cabinet after both my parents were dead. Had to find out that my parents were told that I compartmentalized my mind in times of trauma, or terror, or simple stress. Like a farmer who's tractor turns over on him in the middle of a desolate field and who calmly cuts his leg off with a saw to extricate himself and only goes into shock after he's free.

In the dim and lonesome hallways of my heart, I think I have always known that beyond the truth, the lies, the death and the disappearances, that I am still at fault for so many different things. I've pushed them away for a long time, living under the impression that if I cleared my head, Molly would come back to me.

That is not the truth as she saw it, certainly.

But this is: Molly was my idol. If I believed in anything aside from science, it was that Molly was meant for me and that she was a true angel. If she is dead, maybe she's looking down on me right now and trying to reason with God to get me into heaven. I needed Molly. I needed to possess her. I know that now. I am haunted by every person I have ever loved.

I am sitting in a small cell in Granite Lake drinking coffee from a Styrofoam cup. It has been three days since Sheriff Drew shackled my hands together and told me I needed to be a gentleman, that for the sake of everyone involved I needed to cooperate. At night, I dreamt of Molly. We'd sit beside one another on the dock and talk about the future, about Katrina, about the nameless children we would have in the years to come. Sometimes, Ginny was one of our children and she would swim in the water at our feet, her tan, lithe body circling like a shark below us.

I am on medication again, Zoloft, which probably accounts for the dreams. I requested that a doctor evaluate me and have been under observation by a fellow named Lecocq out of Spokane. He thinks I am clinically depressed and am a danger to myself and others. I have no shoelaces on my shoes and no belt on my pants. I think the Zoloft is helping me. I think I can remember some of the things I have always forgotten.

Sheriff Drew and his deputies combed the house. They found blood and hair in Molly's bedroom and on clothes and pillows left on the floor. They found a drawing, along with my others, of the body of a woman in what they called – because of the clinical nature of the bones, the veins, the exact dissection of the body that was depicted—a death pose. A woman that resembles my wife.

Leo hired me a lawyer from Spokane who tells me they have nothing, no concrete evidence. He tells me there weren't any large bloodstains found, nothing to indicate a murder. You are allowed to bleed in your own home, he tells me. He says no one has been convicted of murder because of a drawing.

Dr. Lecocq says I need long-term therapy. He says I am hiding things and that I need to address them.

Despite all of these things, I am being released today. After three days, Sheriff Drew and his deputies have found no further evidence that might link me to the disappearance or death of my wife. What they found in the house is circumstantial and not valid enough to hold me.

For hundreds of years men and women have argued over the beginning of the family—about the nature of the first nuclear family. What is it in our brains or our souls that makes us think that males are always the aggressors? What is it that makes a child assume that their father is hurting their mother when they walk in on them making love? Why are the females of our species portrayed as shy, coy, submissive partners in sex? And when they are not the archetype, why are they then cast out—harlots, sluts, Hester Prynne.

I think now that Molly has always possessed me. The mistakes we made were often the choreographed steps that signaled the false start of the human parade. Molly's way of sabotaging me, Katrina, our family.

It is useless for me to blame Molly now. She isn't here to defend herself or to defend me. What remains is my memory and the black spots that drift through my mind, the spots that are beginning to pale a bit, the spots that are becoming translucent and that I am terribly afraid to look through.

"All right, Paul."

I look up from my cup of coffee and see Sheriff Drew standing in front of my cell, unlocking it. He's not wearing his hat and his face shows a growth of gray beard. There are circles beneath his eyes. He looks sad.

"Can I have my belt?" I ask.

"Can't give that to you until we check you out up front," he says. "Policy, I'm afraid."

"Is Ginny here?"

"Yep," he says, opening the door. "Bruce drove her and your lawyer friend up in his truck. You'll get to see them in due course. C'mon out now."

I step through into the hallway and Sheriff Drew extends his hand to me. I don't know why, but I take it and we shake.

"You're a troubled person, Paul," Sheriff Drew says. He holds my hand tightly, like he's trying to squeeze air out of it. "I think you've got too much science and not enough sense rattling around in that head of yours. People up here, they don't think like you. Fact is, I don't think anyone thinks like you. I don't know where your wife is, Paul, not a single damn clue. I'll tell you that straight to your face. I hope to God she's somewhere safe."

"So do I," I say.

"I believe you do, Paul," Sheriff Drew says. "I honestly think you love your wife and that you're worried about her. And I think that sometimes you forget things, and you hide things, and you do and say things that I don't quite understand. Does that sound right to you?"

"Yes," I say.

"Then I want you to know something—I don't believe Molly's safe. I believe she's dead somewhere and that you might know where that place is. I also think that you don't have any idea where you might have stuck her; that you know you're half way to crazy and capable of things you've never considered. Does that sound right to you?"

"I've never hurt anybody," I say.

"That may be," Sheriff Drew says, "but I'm going to find out for sure. You can count on that."

IN ANOTHER TIME, in another life, Granite City was heaven. Molly and I had grown tired of Los Angeles and the disappointments we'd encountered there, so when the job opportunity arose in Spokane, it seemed like the ideal situation.

Molly felt at home on the lake; felt for the first time that she could be herself without the constraints of her family looming behind her, questioning her decisions. In the glimmer of a few precious months in the Pacific Northwest, I believe we never loved each other more.

On Saturdays, we'd wake up late and eat our breakfast on the dock. Molly often would fix something different every weekend, a new recipe she'd discovered in a magazine or book, or she'd fill a basket with fruit and bread and a bottle of wine. We'd sit on the dock, our feet dangling into the lake, eating and talking; sometimes we'd merely sit silently, our fingers intertwined, watching the turn of the season.

Sunday nights, we made love. It didn't matter if we'd found reason to argue that day or if one of us was feeling contrary, by the time the sun sloped behind the mountain, we'd resolved to love each other, for better or worse. What was amazing was that it never felt forced or planned.

Come Monday, when I was due back on campus, Molly would wake me with a soft kiss to the back of my neck. "Wake up, baby," she'd whisper into my ear. "It's time for my little boy to wake up."

I'd turn over to face her and she'd smile and kiss my eyes, my ears, the bridge of my nose. We'd hold each other until the last possible moment, until I knew that I'd have to go to work, again, without showering.

True love is a blinding thing, it can color the experiences of even the worst events with a rosy tint, it can turn men and women into the best type of people—ones who will sacrifice the world for a shared moment of bliss.

Despite the pain and the suffering that happened after we fell apart, there is nothing that can replace the memory of a time when we were perfect, a time when we were man and wife, when there were no pills, no anger, no politics of the human heart. It was a moment in our lives that was ruled by faith, love, and hope—and the consequences of believing in all three.

Now, as I sit beside Leo, my friend and lawyer, in the backseat of Bruce Duper's Bronco, I wonder how it could have gone so miserably wrong.

"These people up here," Leo says, "don't have any idea what criminal justice is. My god. Town of morons. The lawyer I got for you in Spokane probably got his degree through the Internet. And that sheriff! Where'd they find him? Central casting?"

Ginny sits stoically beside Bruce in the front of the truck, trying not to listen to Leo. Every few moments she strings her fingers through her hair and then she sighs until it sounds like every part of her body has relaxed. I touch her on the shoulder and for a moment she takes my hand, gives it the smallest squeeze, and then lets go.

"Look," Leo says, "I booked you a flight out of here for tomorrow. Let's get you back to L.A. and some semblance of real life."

"I'm not going back to L.A.," I say. "I need to find Molly."

Ginny turns around in her seat and fixes me with an empty glare, like she can't decide if she's angry or if she's concerned. I wonder how much she knows now about my daughter, about my marriage, about me. "Paul," she says, "please. Do what Leo tells you."

"You don't understand," I say.

"I understand plenty," Ginny says.

"This isn't some kind of movie," I say. "You can't just decide what my motives are because you think it makes a good plot. You can't just say things because you think you should, because you think some actress would."

"Hey, hey," Leo says, patting my thigh gingerly. "We're all in for the good fight here. No one here is against you, Paul."

"Is that true, Leo?" I say. "Is it really?"

No one says anything for a long while until Bruce Duper clears his throat and starts talking.

"I remember when you and Molly first moved up here," Bruce says. "You know what's funny? I remember what you guys were wearing. Paul, you had on a black T-shirt and these tan cotton shorts. Do you remember that? And Molly, God bless her, she was wearing a yellow sundress and had on a straw hat with a wide brim. Like one of those ladies you see in old movies. She was beautiful, wasn't she, Paul?"

"She is," I say.

"You two just looked like movie stars to me," Bruce says quietly. "All I wanted to do was move to California and find a woman like that. Find a woman who would make me look like a movie star. But you know that's just dream stuff. Movie stars don't even look like that anymore. I'll tell you something: everybody on the lake was talking about you folks. You ever seen Molly before, Ginny?"

"Only in pictures," Ginny says.

"Well, a picture doesn't do her justice. She had an air about her, you know? Picture can't capture that." Bruce stares out his side mirror and shakes his head. "I really got to know Molly this past year. Got to understand a lot of things about you and her. And you know what? I think you two forgot how to love each other, and that's just like poison. Worst thing you can do is forget how to love someone.

It makes every part of you rot to shit, if you excuse my language."

"I never stopped loving her," I say. "I'm sorry you have to hear that Ginny, but it's the truth."

"You think I don't know that?" Ginny says. "You think your actions these last few days don't tell me everything I need to know about our relationship? Christ."

"You two are missing the point," Bruce says. "My parents have been married going on forty-five years, and you know what? I don't think a day has gone by when they haven't gotten annoyed or mad at each other, but they always settle everything up by the end of the day. There was always communication. I think you and Molly lost that, Paul."

Ginny is fuming in the front seat. She keeps fidgeting like she wants to turn around and say something to me. But what can she say? She's never been in a place like this, she's never experienced anything that could prepare her for today.

BRUCE PULLS OFF the road at a 76 station to fill up the tank and so Ginny can use the restroom.

"Real spitfire, that one," Leo says. "How old is she? Ten?"

"She's nineteen," I say.

"What's up with her hand?"

"Leo."

"Hey," he says, "I had to ask."

"Listen," I say. "Take Ginny back with you to LA. She doesn't need to stay here."

"Neither do you," he says. "She won't go unless you do. We already discussed this while you were in the clink."

"This isn't her place," I say. "She doesn't belong here."

Leo fiddles with the clasp of the manila envelope that is sitting on his lap. Inside are some of the things Sheriff Drew took from my home. "How long have we been friends, Paul? Fifteen years? Something like that?"

"A long time," I say.

"A long time, right," Leo says. "And you know I've always thought we had a good friendship. I thought Molly was a great girl and Katrina was just a beautiful baby, you know that, right? What I don't understand, Paul, is the stuff that I've been hearing from Bruce and this Sheriff. I mean, I don't want to sound crass here, but you sound like a freaking psycho, buddy."

"Molly and I had our problems," I say. "I handled a lot of things wrong, I admit that. But I never hurt her, not once. You know that, Leo. She was the most important thing in the world to me. Katrina, too."

Ginny walks out of the gas station and I can't help but stare at her. She is a specimen. I never get tired of her face.

"Ginny says you've been acting funny," Leo looks at me. "Says you grabbed her arm and nearly broke it. Is that true?"

"That's not the truth," I say.

"Look," Leo says, and he hands me the manila envelope he's been playing with. "I saw these pictures you drew and I can't make heads or tails of them. Are they organs?"

If I were in Leo's place, I don't think I'd ask any questions. I don't think I'd want to know what goes on in the personal lives of my married friends. If I were Leo, I'd want to believe that a good, normal marriage was still possible. I'd want to think that my friend from college, the guy with the level head, the guy who married young to a great woman, the guy who knew what direction he was going, had all the right answers. Most of all, if I were Leo, I wouldn't ask *me* anything.

"Yes," I say, "and bones. Different things. Renderings of different objects."

"But they're of Katrina and Molly, is that right? I mean, shit Paul, let's just get down to the basics here. You drew the organs and bones of your dead girl and your missing wife, right?"

Ginny and Bruce are standing outside the car talking. Bruce is pumping gas into the tank and Ginny is standing there saying something. She's moving her hands wildly, like she's trying to get something important across to him.

"That's right," I say.

"When did you draw them?" Leo says. "I mean, why the fuck would you do something like that? You know? It's not right, Paul, anthropology aside. You don't just draw the bones of your little girl after she's dead. Are you listening to me?"

My brain feels hurried, frantic, and I'm trying to set things back in time. I can feel it washing over the bad things, the mistakes, clearing away space for the happy memories. I see Molly and me sitting on the dock and then I see Ginny and me making love, *banging*, by the side of the road. I see the day Katrina was born and then I just see whales and diagrams of digs in Africa and there, *there* is Molly, finally, guiding my hand over the thin onionskin paper, etching Katrina's organs, getting the scale correct, referring to the photos. We were her parents. The coroner had to give us the photos.

"I don't know when I drew them," I say.

"You just don't do something like this," Leo is saying, but I'm there with Molly at the table. There are flowers in the center of the table, two glasses of wine, sheets of onionskin. It is daytime. Molly always preferred to work in natural light. I am trying to get the scale correct, trying to make each drawing as perfectly accurate as possible. Each drawing must configure to the one before it. I must maintain the integrity of each scale or else whoever comes behind me might misinterpret my drawings. But this never happened, not exactly. I am confusing time again. Two different days have become one in my mind. The scale of events is all wrong.

"I'm trying to get the scale correct," I say, and when I hear my voice it sounds like a phantom. I didn't mean to say anything.

"I'll tell you the scale of things," Leo says, not understanding that I am having a conversation that is stuck somewhere in time. "I think you need to come to L.A. and get some help. Hire some kid to drive your car back, whatever."

Before I can answer, Ginny and Bruce slip back into the car.

"We all buckled up?" Bruce asks, as though he's taking kids to a baseball game.

"Tight as a bug," Leo says. "Let's just get moving. Get Paul home."

"I'm not flying back, Leo," I say. "I meant it when I said it before. I appreciate you flying up here to supervise my defense or whatever it is you did, but I have to stay here with Molly."

"You know," Ginny says, "you talk like everything is just all right. It's not. You spent three days in jail. That means there's some evidence of *something*, right, Leo?"

"Well, not exactly," Leo says.

"Whatever," Ginny says. "Whatever, whatever, whatever. I just can't even think anymore. This has totally overloaded my faculty for reasoning. Things are not all right, Paul. Don't you get it? Don't you feel anything?"

I do feel something, though I'm not sure exactly what it is. Sorrow? Anger? Relief? I do know that I am not all right. Perhaps I've gone invisible for years at a time, shifting through my home like a spirit. Perhaps I've lived an entire life in someone else's skin, my words and actions invented. Or perhaps I've just disappeared and reappeared at the appropriate times—when my absences would have been least noticeable. The medication Dr. Lecocq gave me in jail seemed to open things up for me: memories, emotions, tiny scenes from my domestic life that I thought had been lost. When I think of myself right now, I see myself like I'm inside an old TV: body floating loosely in space, action surrounding me, lost in a blur of lights and movement. And then the TV begins to fade and my body becomes long and narrow and my head shrinks and shrinks until it is swallowed into a tiny white dot. To Ginny, Bruce, and Leo I must look absurd.

"I've done some things that I don't admire," I say.

"You don't have to tell us anything," Leo says.

"Yes he does," Ginny says. "He has a whole lot of explaining to do to me."

"You don't know anything about me," I say to no one particular, but I mean it for everybody.

"Go fuck yourself," Ginny says.

BY THE TIME we get to Bruce's, the wind has picked up and thick blankets of black clouds are hovering above the lake. The water is rolling with foot-tall whitecaps.

"I don't understand why anybody lives in this state," Leo says. We're getting out of Bruce's truck and the first sprinkles of the day are beginning to fall. "Does it ever stop raining?"

"You'd all better stay here tonight," Bruce says. "No use going out on the boat and getting stuck in a storm."

"That's very generous of you," I say, but Bruce just nods obediently. It's the first time I've spoken in almost thirty minutes.

I look at Ginny and try to smile. Her skin has paled since we arrived here and I think that the sun makes her beautiful. I think that Ginny requires the sun like a plant does: Without it, she would wither and die, a pale, limp twig.

"Do you want to take a walk?" I ask Ginny.

"Are you sick? It's about to pour."

"We won't go far," I say. "I just want to spend some time alone with you. We can talk."

Ginny looks at Bruce and Leo like she needs approval. Neither says anything. She looks up at the sky and shakes her head. "Let me go inside and get a coat," she says.

I CAN'T LINE all of the events up in order, but I am beginning to see them again for what they are.

I've learned things about humans that astonish me. I am able to pinpoint certain places in our collective time-lines when things occurred: We moved from trees, we began hunting with simple tools, we drew pictures on the walls to tell our stories.

We've used pictures to convey everything from love to savagery. We've used them to help discover inner truths.

Molly used pictures to work out the demons, to make the choices she couldn't make in real life. I've used them to demonstrate human life, the variables we have been given. To document discovery. To dissect our existence.

I thought I could figure out what was wrong with Katrina. I thought I could get a better understanding of her body if I looked at it.

I am a scientist, or at least I am training to be one. I am qualified to examine human bones and tissue for anthropological reasons.

"I want to take a sample of Katrina's hair," I said to Molly. It was the fifty-second straight day that the temperature had topped one hundred. "Maybe I can see something from her follicles."

Molly was sitting at her easel, her brush swiping the canvas in rough strokes, as though she were conducting a symphony. She was painting a breast. She'd been painting it for three days, this single disembodied breast.

"You're the doctor," Molly said, not looking at me. "Does this look right to you?" She'd begun to outline the breast with thick, black lines. "Are the proportions correct?"

"Yes," I said, because there were no other words I could possibly say.

I found Katrina sitting out front, her tiny hands buried in the sand. She was wearing a wide-brimmed hat like her mother favored and her face was covered in sun block. Her hair had grown long, well beyond her shoulders, and it fanned out softly against her back.

I sat down beside her.

"What are you doing?"

"Digging," she said, her voice just a whisper. She curled her tongue out of her mouth in concentration, like her mother used to do when she was painting more acceptable objects.

"I want to do something," I said. "It won't hurt. Not even a little. Daddy wants to find out why you don't feel so good."

"The heat," she said. She picked up words and sayings like a magnet.

"I'm just going to take a little piece of your hair," I said and she immediately swung her head around and stared at me. I thought I'd said it gently. "It's not even going to hurt a teensy-weensy bit."

I brought Katrina into the kitchen and set her up on the counter. Her body was covered in cysts and open sores, though when I looked at her I never saw them. I wet a comb and ran it through Katrina's hair, avoiding the lesions that dotted her scalp.

"Cold," Katrina said. "That's chilly."

"Sorry about that," I said.

"Brrr," Katrina said and then she giggled.

"Quiet her," Molly said from the living room.

I used a pair of scissors Molly purchased months before, when she thought she was well, when she thought she might like to sew one day, and I trimmed the loose ends from Katrina's wet hair. When she saw the first locks tumble to the ground, her eyes began to well up with tears.

"Don't cry," I said. "Even Mommy and Daddy get haircuts. You're such a big girl now. Such a little angel."

I scooped up a handful of hair from the floor and placed it in a petri dish filled with iodine.

"You don't have to cry," I said. "Everything is fine. Look." I picked up our teakettle from the stovetop and brought it over so Katrina could see herself.

"I'm round," she said.

"That's just the reflection," I said. "Look at your hair. Isn't it pretty?"

"Like Mommy," she said.

"That's right," I said. "Just like Mommy's."

I set the teakettle down and picked my baby girl up from the counter. She wrapped her arms over my shoulders and hugged me, her damp hair against my cheek. She raised her tiny head and kissed me on my chin, where my stubble is always the softest. "I love you, Daddy," she said.

"My little angel," I said and it was all I could do not to break down in sobs, because I knew then what I know now: that the end had long since been determined.

ELEVEN

"DO YOU LOVE me?" Ginny says. "I mean, is there part of you that actually is still capable of that sort of thing?" We're walking along the narrow beach below Bruce Duper's cabin.

"I don't know if it's possible right now," I say. "Nothing seems solid to me. Like this is a dream we're all having. I know that I feel very strongly for you and that I will love you again. That I need to."

"What does that even mean?"

"It's like a sliver beneath my skin," I say. "I just keep trying to claw it out but I can't force it. It's coming, I think. I really do." I take Ginny's hand, but she wrenches it free.

"That's bullshit," Ginny says. "You've lied to me about everything. You never planned to marry me, did you?"

"We'll go back to L.A. and make it work," I say.

"You think I'm just a little girl," Ginny says. "I'll never be as good as your wife. I'll never give you the same things she did. You're ungrateful, you know. You probably wish I wasn't even here. That's the truth, isn't it?"

"No," I say. I want to tell her that it's like flying with paper wings—that when you're a child, it seems possible—but when you grow up it just sounds doomed for failure. "I want you to be proud of me, Ginny. You're going to have moments in your life where you feel like I do. You won't want people to think you're crazy because you do things they don't like. But that's how I feel and you're not part of it. Not right now at least."

"You let your daughter die," Ginny says.

"I didn't," I say.

"Sheriff Drew said you did," Ginny says.

"We made mistakes," I say. "He doesn't know anything."

Ginny stops walking and glares at me bitterly. "I don't know anything, Paul. You haven't told me a single thing."

I put my hands on her waist and am surprised when she lets me keep them there. "I want to explain things to you now," I say. "I want to fill in the spaces. I just don't feel right dropping it all on top of you." I lean forward and kiss her once on the lips.

"I hate you," she says, her lips still touching mine.

I can feel the heat radiating from her body. She is more alive to me right now than she has ever been. We kiss again and when Ginny closes her eyes, I open mine. I stare beyond her face and see the swirling water and the black clouds. Her hands are in my hair and I feel her eleventh finger.

"I hate you," she says over and over again, her words beginning to lose shape for me. Beyond her words, beyond her face, beyond the rolling lake water and the storm clouds, I know that

Ginny exists for me right now. I know that she is alive and she has emotions and that to her I am something enormous.

Ginny presses herself hard against me and slides her hand down my back, squeezing at my flanks. I close my eyes and Molly is there. We are walking along the Santa Monica Pier. It is summer. Our hands are intertwined and we are swinging them back and forth. The air is warm and breezy and children are running in front of us, eating cotton candy and dragging balloons.

It is an event that never happened.

"I love you," I say, to this vision in my mind.

"Don't say that," Ginny says, pressing me down into the sand. "Don't ever say that again. I won't ever love you."

WE LAY IN the sand talking, our voices calm, rational. We could be discussing the grocery list. The rain falls now in a steady torrent, but the air isn't too cold. Ginny's face is flushed. There is sand in her hair, eyebrows, stuck to her chin. Our bodies are twisted together so that for a moment I don't know whose body I'm touching—everything below my head feels numb, useless, dead.

Ginny props her head on my chest and then tilts it back to catch the rain. I look in her mouth and see her teeth, her gums, her pink tongue. She gulps at the rain like an animal, like she is standing before the last pond in a receding wetland.

I did not kill my daughter.

I made a choice of who could be saved between the three of us and who could be sacrificed. It was a simple task that natural selection would have dictated in a different time. I wasn't well, of course. These are not decisions I would make today.

"It tastes so salty," Ginny says dreamily, like she has forgotten that she doesn't love me.

I was afraid that I wasn't alive. I couldn't feel anything anymore. At night, I would put Katrina to bed and then I would sit beside her, watching her chest heave, her face twitch. I would imagine what she would look like if she were a boy, a different girl, our other children.

"When you get back to L.A.," Ginny is saying, "I'm going to drop out of Pierce and transfer to Valley or Moorpark. I think we'll appreciate each other more that way. We'll have more distance. I think that's important."

"Yes," I say. "Distance and time."

"Are you ready to tell me everything?" Ginny says.

"Yes," I say. "Everything I can remember."

I AM GUILTY of this: I have made my life off the carcasses of the dead.

My parents made the first mistake—I should never have been born. When my mother died at sixty-two after her childbearing and child rearing organs conspired to kill her (ovarian cancer followed by breast cancer finally claimed her), I knew for sure that everything I'd become had been set in motion years before.

As a child, I wanted to be a veterinarian. My parents took a loan out on their home so that I could go to a private school for children adept at science. I rode a bus two hours from Walnut Creek to the Bay Area Science Magnet in Palo Alto in order to spend six hours each day sitting in a classroom with kitchen gloves on slicing through the organs of animals, trying to figure out how each worked. I once tried to rig plastic tubing to the heart of a fetal cat so that I could run water through its veins, but I couldn't make it work. I was encouraged to experiment, to explore my science. But it wasn't about science. It was the feeling of touching the insides of these beasts, of seeing the things they'd never seen, of probing within their bodies, of coming closer to God than I had any right to come.

I became fascinated with finding the roots of man, of trying to see how we had evolved. I yearned to see what was inside of me, to make sense of the feelings and sensations I'd always had. I needed to be able to compare what I was finding in these animals with what I knew was bearing down inside of me: *Why had I ever been born? Why wasn't I a dog, a cat, a possum? What made me any different from these animals?*

The first cut I made on my own flesh was on the backside of my thigh. I was twelve. I carved four squares out of myself and placed them in Zip-loc bags and then buried them beneath a tree for three days. When I dug them back up, my specimens were black and shriveled. I compared my dead skin to the skin of a raccoon I'd found in a text book.

We looked the same.

I kept cutting myself, looking for proof that I was different than the animals I was finding. The more I dug into myself, the more I became obsessed with finding some kind of center. It felt like I could just keep slicing away and nothing would happen.

My mother found me out back with the carcass of a fetal pig I'd brought home from my advanced physiology class. I was seventeen. I'd made an incision along the top of the pig's head and was peeling the skin back over its eyes; just as the book I'd gotten from the library on human pathology described. I was writing notes in my sketchbook about my impressions, my feelings, the way it felt to be so close to the center.

"Good God," she said.

"It's nothing," I said. "It's a homework assignment."

"What did you do to your hair?" she said. I remember her voice sounded hoarse, like she'd been running.

"I shaved it off," I said.

Mom looked down at the pig. "Why do they make you bring these things home?"

"I get extra credit," I said. "They're going to let me be a teacher's assistant next quarter. I'll be helping other kids."

"Where do they get these animals?" my mom asked. She was staring at the lines I'd drawn bisecting the pig's head into hemispheres.

"They're already dead," I said.

My mom lifted up my sketchbook and began flipping through it, through the diagrams of my specimens, my skin comparisons, my conclusions. She stopped at a drawing I'd made years before of her standing in the kitchen. I'd charted the way her words seemed to fall out of her mouth and shatter. I'd broken her words down by the letter, the sound, each word taking on a new significance.

"Paul, what are you?" she said.

"I'm your son," I said, because that was all I could say.

"I thought you stopped all this years ago," she said.

"I never stopped," I said.

"Dr. Loomis told me that you'd grow out of this," she said. "That puberty would fix you."

"I'm trying," I said.

"This ends today," my mom said.

But how can you stop when it's the only thing that makes you feel alive? The only thing that tells you there is a purpose to your life beyond eating, breathing, procreating?

I tried my best to become normal. In college, I joined a fraternity and made friends with people I never would have met otherwise—people not obsessed with science, only obsessed with being college students—and found that if I was distracted long enough, I didn't think about the words and images that had plagued me for so long. I discovered what it meant just to be a kid, just to live life for what it was then: a series of unrelated events that I had no control over; had no chance to wreck.

The error I made was assuming it would always be like that, as long as I kept perspective.

I TELL GINNY about how I met Molly, about how we began dating, about the first time I realized I was in love with her. We were sitting on the floor of her dorm room at UCLA eating pizza. Her hair was long and tied into a ponytail. She was wearing overalls.

"I just looked at her and knew that she was the person I wanted to marry," I say.

"Do you have moments like that with me?" Ginny asks.

"They're different," I say. "I've experienced so many different things that I can't believe in that innocent kind of love anymore. It's just not possible to me. But I never get tired of looking at you."

Ginny frowns in a way that I have come to believe is her way of resigning herself. *This is my life*, it says. *This is the person I have dedicated my life to.*

"Molly was my first," I say.

"But you're mine," Ginny says.

Yes, I think. Perhaps she finally understands that you never outlive your first; that I will haunt her.

The rain begins to turn from a sprinkle into a full shower.

"We should get back," I say.

"They'll be worried," Ginny says, gathering her clothes. "I told them we'd only be gone a few minutes."

I grab Ginny's arm, softly this time, and stop her from putting her clothes back on. "I want you to understand something," I say. "I'm not dangerous. I'd never hurt you. Those drawings you saw—those were from another time. They weren't me. Do you understand what I'm saying?"

"I don't think I've ever understood you completely," Ginny says. "I'm not scared of you. Plenty of people are smarter than me, but I think I can tell when I should fear someone. You're sick, though. That's true, isn't it?"

"I used to be," I say. "When I did those drawings—I don't even remember when I did them—but I was sick and Molly was sick and we missed our little girl so much. I can't explain it all to you yet, because I'm not clear where it all fits. It wasn't me, though. You have to believe that. It wasn't wrong. It was—clinical."

"I don't know what I want to believe about that," Ginny says.

"I guess I'm not terribly proper," I say, "but all you need to believe is the truth."

"You're young for your age," Ginny says. "I always thought adults were supposed to have all these issues worked out by now. Why is it, Paul, that you dump everything together and never unsort it? Do you think that's the right way to live? I don't. I hope I'm not like you when the time comes."

"You have wonderful intentions," I say, but Ginny doesn't hear me over the clap of thunder above us.

BY THE TIME we get back to Bruce's cabin, Ginny and I are drenched.

"Thought you guys might have decided to swim back," Bruce says, handing us towels to dry off with. "I'm gonna broil some salmon here in a bit. You two must be hungry."

"Famished," Ginny says. She starts to towel her hair dry but stops when clumps of matted sand start crumbling onto the floor at her feet. Bruce doesn't say anything. He doesn't have to. I'm not looking for his approval. "I'm going to take a shower upstairs. Is that okay, Bruce?"

"Of course," he says. "Whatever you need to do."

"Where's Leo?" I ask after Ginny has left.

"In the sitting room by the fire," Bruce says. "He's screaming at somebody on his cell phone."

"That's what lawyers do," I say and Bruce smiles faintly. "I appreciate what you said in the car. You didn't have to do that."

"I know," Bruce says. "I didn't say it for your benefit, in case you're curious."

"Even still," I say.

"It's important that everyone remembers who the victim is here," he says.

"I'm going to find her, Bruce," I say. "It's just a matter of time. I'm just not one hundred percent clear on some things, that's all. I've not been well, I guess. It's just confusing right now, but wherever Molly might be I will find her."

Bruce makes a clicking noise in the back of his throat and then slowly shakes his head. "When this storm lets up, I want you out of here," he says. "Ginny and your friend Leo are welcome to stay, but I want you out."

"That's fine," I say.

"I should have called the sheriff the first day Molly didn't come across," Bruce says.

"You had no way of knowing," I say. "You did the right thing by calling me."

Ginny comes to the top of the stairs, a towel wrapped around her. "Bruce," she says, "I can't get the hot water to work. Is there some kind of trick?"

"I'll be right up there," he says, his face all sweetness. When Ginny disappears back into the bathroom, Bruce's face collapses. "You're ruining that poor girl and you don't even care. You think all of us are just here to serve you. I'll tell you something, Paul, I won't let you ruin Ginny like you did Molly."

"You don't know the first thing about Molly and me," I say.

Bruce steps close to my face and for a moment I think he might hit me. "I know something about love and about people," he says. "It's something you might want to learn about, Paul. There are limits, you know. A person can only be pressed so far until they crumble."

I want to tell Bruce that he is right. I want to tell him that the only thing I really know about love is that I can't quantify it. I have no scientific data that supports it. The truth about love is that I only know what I learned from Molly and Katrina, and both of them are gone because of me.

I FIND LEO in the living room sitting beside a roaring fire. His expensive loafers are off and he's got his feet propped close to the flames.

"Bruce wants me out of here in the morning," I say. Leo nods his head like he's been expecting this. He probably has. "I guess he thinks I killed Molly. What do you think?"

Leo leans forward and tugs his socks off. He wiggles his toes free and tries to make himself busy getting the lint out from between them. "I don't know," he says finally. "You're not the same person you used to be."

"I'm beginning to understand that," I say.

"When we were roommates in college I got used to seeing you dissecting baby pigs and crap like that," Leo says. "It didn't bother me. That was your gig. And when you had to bring home bags of fingers and toes to study, that was fine, too. But you never had an emotional investment in the bodies. They were just homework, right?"

"I've always been invested in my work," I say. "No one has ever understood that."

"I'm a lawyer, Paul, and probably not a very good one," Leo says, "but I know this: I'm not defined by my profession. I'm not consumed with torts. You used to have a life outside of human history. You used to be *normal*, for Christ's sake."

"What are you saying, Leo?"

"You scare me. And I'm worried that you might hurt Ginny."

"I'd never hurt her."

"You scare me," Leo says again, "and I don't like to feel that way. I don't know what happened to Molly and I'm not sure I want to. But Sheriff Drew told us about what happened to Katrina, and it was different from what you told me at the time."

"She was sick," I say.

"You let her die, Paul," Leo's voice rises an octave. "Did you and Molly think you could just play God out here? Is that what it was? You think you can make choices about who lives and dies? You can't. You're not allowed that, Paul. You were supposed to be a father to that child. If you'd been in any other town you'd both be in jail for child neglect."

"Don't tell me what I've done wrong," I say. "I know what causes life and death better than you ever will. You can't come up here and tell me that I've made mistakes. *I know what I've done*. I know a little something about cause and effect. I know a little something about genetic mutations. I know how to fix things, Leo. Do you know that? I've made it better for the next child I have. I know how to do things properly now."

"And you believe this?" Leo says. "You actually believe this crap you're spouting?"

"It's the truth," I say, but before Leo can reply his cell phone rings and he starts screaming at the person on the other end.

Here's the truth: I let Katrina die. I let her wither away until I barely recognized her. It didn't matter how many times I looked at her skin, her blood, her hair, I could never figure out how to fix her. Molly and I were genetic mistakes—we never should have tried to breed. We should have recognized that neither one of us were mentally stable or physically able.

But what can you do when there is nothing left to do? When you see your child has no chance to live a long, normal life? That despite her great ability to suck information into her tiny head, she couldn't stop tumors from attacking her organs. Do you subject her to doctors who want to make a name for themselves by "curing" her? Do you convince her that spending every day in a hospital, with all of her activities monitored by a machine, is the best way to live? Do you tell her that Mommy and Daddy love her, but, sorry, we need to leave you here while we go back to our comfortable jobs, homes, friends?

We made a choice. We let her live as she wanted to live.

I am not a doctor, despite my best efforts. But I know this: no doctor was ever able to save me. No doctor ever saved Molly from aborting our children. No doctor was going to save Katrina.

She could have lived another five years, I think, had we lived somewhere besides Granite Lake during that broiling summer. Everything died that summer—Katrina was only the beginning.

It was like I was seventeen again. Nothing seemed to make sense to me anymore: My wife was crazy, my daughter was dead, and I was the only one still standing. I needed to get to the roots of my life. Molly was the only person who ever understood that my obsession with humanity was fixed in my need to understand death. I'd come to believe that every child we'd ever conceived was just another experiment in grief and sadness, another reason to believe that nothing was worth loving.

I needed to understand why I was the only one left.

I needed to bring them back to me.

Katrina died in the morning. I dressed her in red OshKosh overalls. I placed hemlock cones and pine needles in her pockets, a strawberry lollipop in her shrunken hand, her favorite stuffed bear beneath her right arm.

"I don't believe in God," Molly said. She was kneeling beside me, shivering.

"It's nature," I said. "God had nothing to do with this."

"Can you make her come back?" Molly said.

"I don't know how," I said.

"That's bullshit," Molly said softly, like she believed it. Like she thought I was holding back on her. "You can do it, I know you can," she said.

"No," I said.

"Yes," she said and started pounding on my back and shoulders with her balled fists. "Yes you can. I know you can. You told me scientists could bring back dormant cells from the Ice Age! They're raising that mammoth, aren't they? They can do it. They can bring her back."

"This is our daughter," I said and then grabbed Molly's arms. She slumped against me, her body folding like a hand puppet.

"She has cells just like anything," Molly said. "We can keep her. We can hold onto her until it's possible. We can do that. We can do that."

"She was wrecked from the start," I said. "It would be just the same."

I stood there for hours watching Molly fuss over Katrina's body. She brushed Katrina's hair with long, slow strokes, making sure each hair was smooth and soft to the touch; all the while whispering softly into Katrina's tiny ears. Molly touched Katrina's face gently, as though she were afraid she might break her, and placed small kisses over her closed eyes. She did all of the things she never did when our child was alive.

"I can't remember loving her," Molly said. "I can't remember her first words. I can't remember talking to her. When did I forget everything?"

"She's dead," I said.

"What happened to me?" Molly stopped brushing Katrina's hair and stared at me, like I knew all the right things to say. Like I knew how to tell her that she had gone crazy. "What happened to us?"

"I can bring her back," I said. "I can do it. It will take time. But we have plenty of that now. We have all the time in the world. We'll do it just like man started. We can simulate everything. We can take her to the Galapagos Islands. They have animals there that don't exist anywhere else. Evolution is just starting there. We could take her cells there and put them in the water. Just let them grow. We could do that. We can do it, Molly. I can bring her back."

The awful truth is that I believed all of this. Now, sitting with Leo beside the fire, it seems preposterous. Leo is talking to someone about an insurance settlement, like he's forgotten everything that I represent is still only inches from him.

I stare into the fire and watch the flames lick at the stack of wood—as though they know exactly what they are doing, what they were born to do. The logs burn orange and yellow, and plumes of dark gray smoke are wafting into the air. I think that the colors are pleasing and warm and that they know something. They have a purpose. A direction. They climb higher and higher in the fireplace, crackling and hissing pleasantly. I lean forward to warm my hands, to see if I can feel anything anymore.

My mind is unfolding, smoothing out the creases in my memory, lining things back up.

I can't feel anything. I close my eyes and lean closer.

It was impossible. It would have taken millions of years. It would have required too many elements, too many degrees of difficulty.

I am beginning to feel something again.

"What the fuck's that smell?" Leo says. His back is to mine.

I would have needed to harness everything I'd ever learned, plus powers I've never had. It was impossible.

"Oh shit," Leo says and then he's on top of me, pounding his hands on my shirt, my face, my hair.

TWELVE

"WERE YOU TRYING to hurt yourself?" the EMT asks me. He's sitting on the floor of Bruce Duper's living room wrapping my hands with gauze.

"No," I say. "I fell asleep."

"In front of the fire?" the EMT says. "You just fell asleep sitting in front of the fire with your hands outstretched?"

"I guess so," I say. "I've been under quite a bit of stress."

The EMT shakes his head like he can't believe someone as stupid as myself exists and then continues wrapping me. I've sustained some minor burns, nothing requiring hospitalization. My eyebrows are gone, however, and my bangs are scorched. My hands are bubbled with blisters and they ache, but the EMT says the damage is nothing compared to what would have happened had Leo not been here.

"All right," the EMT says, "you're going to want to keep your hands moisturized with aloe vera and vitamin E. Change the gauze every six to eight hours."

"Will he scar?" Ginny asks.

"Only mentally," the EMT says and starts packing up his supplies.

There's a knock at the front door so Bruce excuses himself; when he comes back a few moments later, Sheriff Drew is beside him.

"Heard the nine-one-one call," Sheriff Drew says, "wanted to make sure everything was okay out here."

"Just dandy," Leo says, immediately going into lawyer mode. "Nothing for you to see here, Officer."

"I'm not an officer," Sheriff Drew says. "I'm a sheriff, and I'd appreciate it if you took pains to remember that."

Leo doesn't say anything; instead he just salutes Sheriff Drew. "Okay, Leo," I say. "Sheriff Drew is just doing his job."

"You're right, Paul," Sheriff Drew says, but there is nothing friendly in his voice. His time for caring and compassion has long since passed.

"Unless you've got another warrant," Leo says, "I'd like you to leave my client alone. Your behavior is bordering on harassment and I'm not opposed to suing you, believe me."

"No need for that, I'll just make my way on out of here," Sheriff Drew says and then turns to leave. Before he's walked three steps, though, he stops and turns back around. "You're an anthropologist, right, Paul?"

"Don't answer him." Leo says.

"I am," I say.

"Then maybe you can help me out here," the sheriff says. "I've been having a debate with the forensics guy upstate. He says luminol can show blood evidence from, gosh, fifty years ago if conditions are right. He says that even if someone spilled pools of blood and cleaned them up with bleach and soap and, God, just about any kind of cleanser, the luminol would still be able to detect the blood. I say there's no way that's true. What's your take?"

"Don't answer that," Leo says.

"He's right," I say.

"God damn it, Paul," Leo shouts. "You're going to be hearing from my office, Officer Drew. We'll take you for every God damn penny you're worth! Do you hear me?"

"I'll save you some time." Sheriff Drew reaches into his pocket and pulls out a handful of coins and tosses them onto the floor. "You can call me when you have a license to practice in this state."

Before Sheriff Drew has even walked out the front door, my hands are already bleeding again. The EMT, who's been watching the proceedings as though it were network TV, just starts rewrapping my hands without saying a word. Before he goes, he tells me not to clench my fists so tightly for the next two weeks or so.

THE FOUR OF us eat dinner in near silence. Leo is so angry with me, however, that every few minutes he says, "Damn," under his breath and then shakes his head. The only other sounds come from outside, where the wind is howling and a fierce rain is pounding the lake. My hands throb with a dull ache that I am certain will turn into sharp pain once the six Advil I have taken begin to wear off.

The truth is that luminol can show traces of blood evidence for as long as the evidence remains visible through infrared light. Forensic anthropologists have used luminol on the Shroud of Turin, inside Egyptian tombs, and have even used it with some success on ancient burials found in Africa that date back to the Neanderthal era.

"I'm sorry," I say to Leo.

"Don't be sorry," he says, "be smart."

"Give him a break, Leo," Ginny says. "Hasn't he been through enough today?"

"You're right," Leo says, standing up. He takes his napkin and crumples it up into a ball and tosses onto his plate. "You are absolutely right, Ginny. Paul has been through enough to last a lifetime. All of our lifetimes. And you know what? I say, God bless Paul! I say, give the guy a hand for setting himself on fire and then for allowing the local law to harass him and prod him and then provide expert testimony."

"I'm sorry," I say again. "I don't think anything I said has done anything. I just answered his question. I didn't admit to anything but the truth."

"How's that for a change," Leo mutters. "I'm going to go upstairs, swallow a couple of Valium, and pray that when I wake up tomorrow all of this is a dream. Wouldn't that be great?

"Listen to me," Leo says. "I'm losing my mind out here. I'll see you all in the morning."

After Leo leaves, Bruce quietly gets up and starts clearing the table.

"Let me help," Ginny says.

"That's all right." Bruce dismisses Ginny with a wave of his hand. "Sometimes I like to do a little washing and drying. Makes me feel like I've got a family."

Ginny stares at me from across the table. Bruce is already in the kitchen sloshing about in the sink. "I was thinking about you and me," she says, answering a question I have not asked. "I was thinking about how I don't know why I love you. I guess that's funny to be thinking about after all of this, but it's true. I was watching you there, getting your hands wrapped up by that paramedic, and it was like I was watching a little boy."

"That's not a reason to love me," I say.

"No," she says. "It really isn't, is it? I'm a young woman, you know, and I'm not stupid like you might think sometimes."

"I don't think that," I say.

Ginny laughs. "Paul," she says, "I'm not blind. You didn't bring me up here because you love me, did you?"

I don't know how to answer her. It's like she's trying to appeal some verdict. Like she knows every pure and vile thought I've ever had.

"No," she continues, "of course you didn't. None of this is about me, is it? You brought me up here because you think I make you look better, because you look plausible with me on your side. Just some other guy having a midlife crisis. Is that right, Paul? Do you think that is why you brought me here?"

"You were never just a cause," I say.

"I guess not," she says.

"I wanted you from the first time I saw you," I say.

"Why?"

I try to think back to the first time I saw Ginny. I try to remember how it was that we ended up having sex in the backseat of my Honda. I try to think of something I can say that will make Ginny stop this conversation, because I know it is going to end with one of us crying.

I try to think of a lie. Any lie. I try to think of something that will make her cry with joy instead of with anger, sadness, and disappointment.

I tell her the truth instead.

"You reminded me of Molly," I say.

"I don't love you anymore," Ginny says, but she is not crying and she is not kissing me like when she said this before. Her voice is flat and dry. I look at her face, at her skin, at the way her lips come to a sharp point in the center. I try to burn her face into my mind, so that I could sketch it if I had to, so that I could document the moment she realized I would always let her down.

"Maybe you should go back to L.A. with Leo in the morning," I say.

"You're a monster," she says.

"If that makes you feel better," I say, "that's fine. Do what you have to do to forget me. I'll always appreciate you coming up here with me during what must be a very difficult time for you."

"What did you do to your daughter?"

It comes to knowing this: The cry of a newborn baby is the most beautiful sound. The sound of that first cry can never be replicated, can never be charted or quantified by a scientist. It is the only true, pure thing that exists.

"I was a good parent," I say. "I was a great provider for her. You don't know how I struggled for that girl. She was a fight from the start. You don't know about that. You don't know what it means to fight for something, to really go to battle for something you want, do you? You don't know about how man has struggled over centuries to perfect the family. I did what I thought was best for Katrina. I let her live. What would you do if your daughter was sick, Ginny? If she couldn't live in this world without being hooked up to machines to sustain her, if, with every breath she took, there was another X percentage chance that she would catch some new infection? If I could have, I would have preserved her like a monument, I would have made her live for generations, so everyone could appreciate her. But I couldn't, Ginny. I couldn't do that. I couldn't make her. They wouldn't let me and I couldn't do it and I would for her, I would. I would have done anything for her."

My eyes are closed now, and behind them I see Katrina and me running through the woods, her body limp in my arms. Sheriff Drew is behind me and he's shouting, like Ginny is shouting right now, to stop, just stop, please stop, please. But how can I when I know that there is nothing left for me in this world? That all I've created is gone, that Katrina is dead, Molly is missing, and Ginny is leaving.

I squeeze my eyes tighter and fireworks burst into the darkness, orange and blue and yellow gusts of light. I hear my voice behind the lights, behind Ginny's shouting. I'm saying, "I thought I could plant her like a seed in the ground. I thought that."

For two and a half years I thought I could heal my daughter, thought that the dermoid cysts that covered her body in the end could be removed. Thought that whatever was inside of her, whatever was eating her away could be stopped. The truth is that I thought we would be able to strip away the illness from our daughter so that one day she would be entirely new, entirely different, the healthy living child of my dreams.

"Where is she, Paul," Ginny is saying now, through tears and coughs. "What did you do with your wife?"

I told Molly that one day we could bring her back. I told Molly that one day she would love me again, that after all the pain and suffering, there was still a piece of us remaining— another vestigial part of our former selves.

"I don't know," I say.

What I know is that I should never have tried to find the center of things, never should have placed my wife and daughter under a microscope, never should have believed that I was anything other than a husband and a father.

"Did you hurt her?"

"I don't know," I say.

Katrina *was* the child of my dreams: I used to dream, when Molly was pregnant with Katrina, that Molly was in labor and that doctors and nurses were assembling around us. There were bright lights, beeping machines, good cheer. Then, one after another, our other children came springing from Molly. Our ectopic, our abortion, and finally Katrina. I'd wake up to the sound of my own voice and Molly would soothe me back to sleep. She'd say, "You're dreaming, Paul. Everything is fine. We are going to have a beautiful child. She'll paint and draw and love science and she'll be smart. She'll know everything. And she'll have kids, and they'll have kids, and we'll grow old around a huge family. Now, sleep, Paul. Sleep."

It's like I've been asleep ever since.

"You tell me, Ginny," I say. "You tell me what I've done. Because I can't remember anymore. I can't decide if this is real or if I'm going to wake up in my bed and be seventeen again. It's like I've never left here. Like every time you open that mouth of yours, every thing tilts to one side. So you tell me: what have I done?"

I don't know when it happened, but Bruce and Leo are standing next to Ginny now. She's shaking and crying. I remember: My eyes have been closed. Everything seems so bright in here now, like the lights have been turned up, like everything is getting clearer.

"What the hell's your problem?" Bruce is saying, repeating it like a mantra.

"That's what I'm trying to figure out," I say.

Ginny starts gagging, as if she might vomit, then stops and fixes her eyes on me. She doesn't say anything, no one does. The three of them stand there in the too bright light staring at me. I want to close my eyes again and open them back up and be in the cabin with Molly and Katrina and all of this is a nightmare.

"I'm going to leave in the morning," I say.

"I think that's a good idea," Leo says.

BY THE TIME I get up to our bedroom, Ginny is almost completely packed.

"I guess you're going, too," I say.

"No reason to stay," she says. "You've made *that* pretty clear."

"Let me at least pay for your ticket," I say.

"I don't want anything from you anymore," she says. "Leo was nice enough to put it on his credit card. He said I could pay him back whenever I got a chance."

"He's been a good friend to me," I say, but Ginny doesn't respond. She's packing her camera and several notebooks into her backpack. "I'm sorry this had to happen like this."

"Just don't speak," Ginny says. "For ten minutes, just keep your mouth closed."

I think then that I've misdiagnosed everything about Ginny. She is stronger than I've ever been.

Despite it all, Ginny still lets me sleep next to her in bed.

"It's all right," I say. "I can go downstairs and sleep on the couch."

"We're adults," she says and I believe her. I believe that maybe Ginny is old inside and aging with every moment.

"I appreciate you," I say.

"I woke up this morning feeling pretty good," Ginny says. "That was fifteen hours ago. I have to be smart about things. Really just decide what my limits are. This is astounding, Paul. And astounding things don't happen to me everyday. Maybe they used to, when I was a kid. I won't be this age forever, you know, so maybe I'll look back at nineteen and think that this was a watershed year. Do you think it's possible that I'll have another year like this?"

"I don't remember nineteen," I say.

"No," she says, "I suppose you're too far removed from this sort of talk. Would all of this have been better if I were twenty-five? What about thirty-seven? Are those good numbers?" I think Ginny is going to laugh, but she doesn't. Instead, she pulls back the covers on the bed and slides in fully clothed, as if she's afraid her body will somehow deceive her brain and will allow itself to warm me, to hold me. But it's impossible: her body can't work independently of her brain anymore. She knows too much.

I slide in beside her, wearing just pajama bottoms, and for a long time I wonder if this is how it would feel if Molly and I shared a bed again. I look at Ginny out of the corner of my eye and she seems alien to me. Her eyes are closed and her breathing is short and moderated in a perfect replication of sleep. I turn on my side and face her. I place my hand in the vacant space between us and I can feel the heat radiating from her body. She flinches when I touch her arm.

"Are you asleep?"

Nothing.

I look at my watch. The minutes I felt passing have somehow accelerated: We've been in bed for an hour.

"The truth is that doctors found something inside Katrina that changed how I look at life," I say. "You might not want to believe me, but its true. When they did her autopsy they found hair inside her brain tumor, and bone fragments. Do you know what that means?"

Nothing.

"She was doing it herself," I say. "She was trying to find a way to live! It's true, Ginny. It is the absolute truth."

Nothing.

I take my hand from Ginny's arm and turn over onto my back. She doesn't want to hear me, which is fine. I've done too much to make her think I am speaking the truth. But what's funny is how good it feels. I think about the times when I didn't have to lie, when it wasn't my nature to mislead everyone, including myself.

There were times when I was a young man when I didn't think I would ever grow old. I'd find myself in the middle of physiology class poised over the organs of a frog or fetal cat, my hands dirty with dried blood and tissue, and I couldn't be sure how I'd gotten where I was; wasn't absolutely positive I hadn't killed the animal with my own hands. It was in those times that I thought I might just kill myself and never know it, that I'd wake up dead.

I remember the day I told my mother that I was afraid of myself. It wasn't too long after she'd found me with the fetal pig. We were sitting at the kitchen table cutting strawberries.

"Don't tell your father that," she said, fingering the cross that hung around her neck. "It would break his heart." She got up then and started walking around the room slowly, watching each of her steps intently. It was as if she thought she could just stomp my words out of her head. "It's a lack in you," she said rather suddenly. "You've never known how to be a regular boy. Never wanted to play sports or drink beer or fix cars. Why do you think that is, Paul? Did we make some mistake with you?" She walked out of the kitchen and into the living room. I followed her.

She circled the couch twice and then just stopped in the middle of the room. I could smell her from where I was standing: strawberries and baby powder perfume.

"Don't cry," I said. "I don't want you to do that."

"You'll break his heart," she said and I felt sorry for her. All these years she'd tried to raise me, tried to give me some sense of value, some sense of God and church and all I had become was a boy who was afraid of himself—a boy who hurt things. No one wants to raise a wicked person.

"We just won't tell him," I said. "We'll act like I never said anything, okay Mom? We can do that, can't we?" Right then, I wanted to fold my entire life up and throw it away. I wished that I'd never even opened my mouth, wished that I could spin the world backwards to catch up with myself fifteen minutes earlier. I would've said, "Stop, Paul. Just keep cutting strawberries. Just go into your room and do pushups, situps, lift weights." And suddenly, I felt afraid of my mother and what she might say next and what I might say back to her. Because I felt if I said the wrong thing that I would ruin something in her forever, and that a piece of me would just shrivel up and die and I would never be the same again. I wanted to turn around and run out the front door and just keep going, but I couldn't move. It wouldn't matter where I went, anyway, because I would forever have this moment in my head, I could never run far enough away.

I decided then that what people think is true is often better than what the truth *is*. From then on people would only get what sounded best being true about me, no matter the consequence.

Though I think now that that was the wrong thing to do, the wrong philosophy to subscribe to. My mother and father would have thought so, too, if they'd been given the opportunity to choose my beliefs. Because the truth is that they knew all about me, as any good parents surely must. And they were good parents, despite me.

But that day, that wretched day, all I understood was that I needed to make a change, or else I might just collapse my family.

"He can't ever find out," Mom said. "We'll put you back into therapy. Yes. That's what we'll do. I'll tell him you felt like you needed it. And that will be fine, and this time maybe we can fix you. Are you a bad person, Paul? Do I need to be afraid of you?"

"No," I said. "I'd never hurt anybody."

"I guess I should have known about all of this happening," she said. She was still standing in the middle of the room. "It's probably all just in your mind, anyway. And you can't control your thoughts. You probably shouldn't even attempt that, at your age. There is always something else going on that could divert you. I get lost in work sometimes, which helps. I just concentrate on working, make it my life for those nine hours. You should try that, yes, that's something you should attempt." I sat down without saying anything. Mom went to the window in the living room and looked out. She was still a young woman then, only in her forties, but I thought that she suddenly seemed very old to me, like this conversation had slipped twenty years off her life.

"Maybe you should take a nap," I said. "Rest before dinner. You look tired to me."

My mom put a hand up against the window and shook her head deliberately. "I think it's colder this year," she said. "Do you think that? That this year is a touch cooler than last?"

"I don't know," I said.

"You get these ideas in your head," she said, and it was as if she was floating between two conversations, "and it seems like it's your whole life. Everything seems so important. It can ruin things, Paul. It can ruin whole lives."

"I can change," I said. "I think this has helped."

"Do you believe that?" my mother asked.

My mother was staring at me and for one of the first times in my life, I felt like an adult. Her voice was very calm, so I just said, "Yes, I do."

"Thank you," she said.

When my father got home a few hours later, we were both still in the living room, my mother silent and poised by the front window, me sitting in a large overstuffed chair thinking about death and redemption and about my problems and about what my own children would be like and how I would raise them.

"The hell's going on in here?" my dad said. "There's a bunch of rotting strawberries in the kitchen."

Mom didn't say anything then, she just walked past my father and into the kitchen where I heard her turn on the sink and then the small black-and-white TV she kept on the counter. I looked at my watch and saw it was six thirty. The *700 Club* was on.

"What the hell is going on here, Paul?"

"I want to go back into therapy," I said. "See Dr. Loomis again."

Dad sat down on the couch across from me and sighed deeply and then a queer look crossed his face, a look I would see again after my mother finally passed on from the cancer, a look of honest relief. "Well," he said, "I think that's fine. I think that's real fine. Whatever makes you feel right, son. We'll do whatever we can. Mother and I support you one hundred percent."

THIRTEEN

I OPEN MY eyes and look at the clock. It is one forty in the morning. Ginny is asleep, one of her arms draped across my chest. She has taken off her pants sometime during the night, probably in her sleep, and they are balled up at my feet.

Watching Ginny sleep makes me think that there still is a conviction in me that life is worth living, that there is hope for all the beautiful things. Because Ginny is beautiful in her own precious way, and maybe she doesn't really know it, which is fine. Maybe I've made mistakes that are irreversible, maybe I've seen things that I can't unsee, but what remains in me is that life is valuable—that we've all worked terribly hard to perfect this model, that *Homo sapiens* are the only successful branch of our family tree. It isn't humanity that has failed me.

I peel Ginny's arm from my chest and place it beside her. My hand smarts. She stirs a bit, swallows twice, and then continues to snore lightly from her nose. If the truth be known, I wanted to hurt her. I wanted to make her hate me, wanted to show her things that would claim her for the rest of her life. I wanted to run to her and have her reject me for all that I am worth, but she's always been there, always tried to see me as something more than I am. And so she says she doesn't love me. All that means to me is that she once did and that she could again.

The truth about Katrina is this: she was a rare child, even in death. What the pathologists in Granite City said were brain tumors, were actually our children. What the pathologists didn't understand, nor wished to figure out, was that Katrina was a vessel. In her medulla oblongata was a *fetus in fetu*, three inches long, formed of bone, hair, and a mass of macerated embryo.

The pathologists in Granite City didn't know what it was, thought that it was just an anomaly, that it was nothing. They were not students of human history, they were technicians, they were bored technicians cutting apart a child they didn't care about. What they had missed was so obvious: that Katrina had died not from malignancies, not from the dermoid cysts, not from the heat, not from the neglect at the hands of her parents, but that she was doomed from birth.

A week before she died, Katrina's abdomen had begun to swell. She didn't seem to be in any more pain than usual, but each day her side would expand. I kept a chart that Sheriff Drew confiscated with the drawings that detailed the swelling. On the first day it grew 1.5 centimeters. On the second day it grew 1.8 centimeters and so on. When the pathologists sliced her open, violated her sanctity, they said there was a tumor beneath her last rib on the left side. They didn't bother to dissect it. The tumor in her brain had killed her, they said.

But had they bothered to look, had they bothered to really examine Katrina, they would have seen that the tumor behind her rib, in a pocket against the transverse colon, was formed of skin, fat, sebaceous materials, and two pieces of bone that any physical anthropologist would have been able to tell was the superior maxilla. They were technicians. They were underpaid. They didn't care.

It wasn't their little girl.

She was my little girl and I took the time to find out everything about her. I wish I'd done it before she was already dead.

I lean over and kiss Ginny lightly on her forehead. She reaches out to me and rubs my arm. She is still asleep, still dreaming, but her body is reacting the way it always has. Her body doesn't remember that she's lost all emotions toward me.

"Good-bye," I say softly into Ginny's ear.

"Okay, honey," she says, and it sounds sweet and tender and adult and like she's never known how lost I've felt, how I've always been defined by the people who have loved me, how I should have loved every inch of her giving soul.

I slide out of bed and dress quietly in the dark, which is difficult with my hands wrapped in gauze. I peek out the window in our room and see that the wind has settled some and that the rain has stopped. It occurs to me, like a picture slowly being undrawn, that this lake has always held some mystery for me. At first, I thought life here would solve everything, would give me the ability to tell the truth, would give me a family and would cure Molly.

Ginny coughs in her sleep and then sits up, eyes wide open.

"Are you jumping?" she says. She is still asleep.

"You're dreaming," I say.

"Yes," she says. "Do you think I've taken good care of you?"

"The best," I say, then, "go back to sleep," and she does.

It's not the things that I can't change that bother me anymore. My time in jail proved that. I've accepted a few things in the last four days, chief among them being that I can only find Molly by myself, that she is there in our house, and that when I find her she will still love me and that though her heart has been broken by me, I think I can bend it, twist it, and make it mine again. For better or worse.

I tiptoe out of the room and into the hallway, where it is colder and darker. I hear the sound of a toilet running, so I stop outside the door and wait a moment. Bruce Duper comes out of the bathroom at the end of the hall, his body backlit in dull yellow light. His hair is disheveled and he's dressed only in his boxers. I can see his belly and his thick, stout legs, and I think that he is not an animal, he is all guy. He stops there in the light and turns around.

"That you back there, Paul?"

"Yes," I say.

"Why didn't you say something?"

"I didn't want to scare you," I say. It's as though he doesn't know he's wearing mostly skin.

"You going somewhere?"

"I'm leaving," I say.

"Back to California?"

"Don't know," I say and it occurs to me that maybe Bruce sleepwalks, that maybe this conversation is all going to be forgotten.

"I do believe I loved your wife," Bruce says after a time.

"I know," I say.

"You don't know anything," Bruce says.

"Did you get her that new engine for the boat?" I ask. "That Johnson?"

Bruce reaches back into the bathroom and flips the light switch off. He stands at the opposite end of the hallway, shrouded in darkness, like a gunfighter. He doesn't say anything, but he coughs a few times, clears his throat, sighs. "She was practically marooned out there," he says finally. "I liked helping her out when I could." His voice sounds weak and tired, like mine. "That boat you two bought was a real piece of crap, you know. Wasn't worth half what you paid for it. My dad really gave Jersey Simpkins hell for ripping you off. Just let him have it."

"Your dad was good people," I say.

"You can't just leave a woman out there," Bruce says. "She didn't know how to fix a damn thing."

"I'm sure she appreciated your help," I say.

"You know what bewilders me?" Bruce says. "She still loved you. Still thought you two might have a chance. Thought that one day she'd just wake up a young, well woman again. And that wasn't going to happen. You know that. Don't you?"

"I don't know anything," I say.

"She told me that you couldn't race an avalanche. Damndest thing I've ever heard a woman say. But you know, I think she had a point," Bruce says. "It's sure surprising how fast the world can turn upside down, isn't it?"

I stay quiet.

Bruce starts to sniffle. "Oh hell," he says and then he plops down against the wall. "Like a big old baby."

I walk down the hall and sit beside Bruce. "You must be cold," I say. "You should just go back to bed." I see that tears have cut rough canals through Bruce's beard. His eyes are closed and his shoulders are heaving. I want to embrace him, to tell him how sorry I am, how sad I am, and how we will get through all of this together.

But there is none of that in me. There is no diagram for grief between Bruce and me. Because the truth is that I didn't know Bruce loved Molly, didn't think the world could exist with more than one person loving Molly, didn't think that anyone was entitled to those emotions aside from me.

"Just get the hell out," Bruce whispers. "Don't you ever come back here. Don't you ever say another nice thing about me or my family or about anyone here on this lake. It's not your right anymore. It's not your provenance. You just disappear forever. Let us all forget about you. Can you do that for me, Paul? Can you let me have this place without you? Can you let me have Molly to myself now? You don't deserve her. Maybe you did once, but that was different. You were different."

I don't answer because I don't know what I could possibly say, don't know how to respond to a man who feels honestly about me, feels that I am dangerous, feels that I am different than I used to be.

Bruce stands up then, as though he hasn't spoken, as if we hadn't had this entire conversation, and says, "I'm nearly naked out here. I'm god-damn half naked out here."

"You should go on back to bed," I say.

Bruce pauses there in the hallway. Black hair covers his body like vines, and for a moment he scratches his sternum like he's trying to dig the roots out. "You ever broken a bone, Paul? Ever felt your body snapping?"

"Yes," I say. "More than you know."

"That's how Molly said she felt all last month," Bruce says. "Like you were breaking her in two every day."

"It was the anniversary of Katrina passing," I say. "Its always a tough time for both of us. Maybe you can't understand that. I hope you never have to."

"She felt you watching her," Bruce says. "She said she could feel you in her bones."

Yes, I think, I have always watched her. I have traced her throughout time and conceived her creation, her demise. I have counted the seconds between her breaths, predicted within five the amount of times she blinks in a given minute. I have seen her through the window of our home, when she didn't know she was being seen, crying for a life she could never control.

"That's preposterous," I say.

"Is it?" Before I can answer, Bruce shuffles slowly back to his bedroom and closes the door softly behind himself. I hear his bare feet scuff along the floor, hear his bed squeeze down beneath his weight, and then all I hear is my own breathing, steady and full and I wonder this: How long has it been since the last time I was home?

OUTSIDE, THOUGH THE wind and rain have died, the air is cold and damp and I think that this is how it has always been for me. That no matter how many times I've tried to reach the center of myself, the truth about what makes me who I am, what makes me human, I always end up here, in the dark, cold and wandering. Where is the difference between man and animal? Why am I not a monkey, a pigeon, a raccoon? What causes me to be human on the outside and yet so feral and animal on the inside?

I'm standing beside Bruce Duper's boat, the *Angel Mine*, and all I can do is wonder at myself. Wonder at the way I'm about to head out into the lake, back to my home, back to my Molly—and for what? I know this now for certain: I have never left here. And I know this: I have been back here recently. The thing that makes me different from an animal, the result of being the child of loving human parents, is my ability to reason. And though reason has left me at times, for long periods, for years I think, I know that it has come back to me now, tonight, on this lake in front of this boat with miles of water between myself and the truth.

I step into the *Angel Mine* and find beneath the captain's chair a life jacket that fits me. I turn the key that's in the ignition and the motor comes on easily with not so much a roar but with a hum. The running lights flash on around the base of the boat and shroud the marina in an odd orange glow. I look behind me, to where Bruce Duper's house is, and see a single light on upstairs. There is a figure in the window, like a ghost, and for a moment I think I see it waving at me, but it is too far away and much too dark. I raise my hand up and wave back anyway, in case whoever it is can see me, or in case it is a ghost and it needs confirmation that I am haunted.

It has not always been the people I have loved who have haunted me—there have been the people I have never known who have also crept into the small spaces. From that day when I told my mother that I was afraid of myself, the apparition of who I could have been has visited me, has sat on the edge of the bed and snickered. *What you could have done*, it says. *The people you could have saved!*

I've tried to define that lack in me that my mother saw, that difference that caused me to be here, now, on this boat, cutting across a blackened lake on the 22nd day of September. I stare up into the sky and see the moon shining dully through the clouds. It will be the day of the Autumnal Equinox when the sun rises in a few hours, and I know that I will be defined not by what the sun finds, but by what I must locate, what I must discover.

I slip my hand into my pocket and pull out a Zoloft, the medication Dr. Lecocq gave me in jail. The pill is small and round, its edges perfected by a machine somewhere in the Midwest, and I swallow it without any water. This is not the first time I've taken medication. The truth is that I never should have stopped, should never have deemed myself healthy. Dr. Loomis put me on Ritalin when I was twelve, and again when I was seventeen, and maybe it made me calmer, less afraid, but it never was able to solve the riddles I've had—was never able to fill in the black spots of time that I'd lose. The Zoloft, however, is starting to do the trick again, causing the moments in my life that I've stored away to reappear, to come dripping into my mind.

Bruce's boat runs faster than our old Whaler used to, seems to understand the way the small waves curl, and slides over them with something less than patience. Before I am completely aware, I see that I'm already halfway home. I lay back on the throttle and the boat slows to a crawl. The water looks glassy and sharp. I think about the days Molly and I spent out on the water, the nights we made love, actually created love, in the dank cabin of the Whaler. We would lie there, our bodies intertwined in the dark, listening to nature.

"How do you think we came from the sea?" Molly said

once. Her head was on my chest and we hadn't spoken yet, hadn't bothered to ruin the silence.

"It's a long process," I said. "Single cell life to, you know, the guy you see at Safeway, was complicated by a billion factors. I think probably it all came down to need. Food, shelter, sex, a combination of everything." I ran my fingers through Molly's hair. She hummed softly, like a cat.

"But why?" she said. "Why leave something so beautiful for something so ugly, so malformed, so dangerous? It doesn't make sense to me, to leave the kind of serenity of the water."

"There are predators everywhere," I said.

Molly laughed then, this was before she was really sick, and sat up. "This whole thing," she said, "this whole, *Earth* thing—you know what I mean? This whole planet is here for what? To serve us? To serve you and me and our unborn babies? Do you think that is why it's here?"

"I think we're bacteria on a big rock," I said.

"That's not enough of an answer. What if one of your students raises her hand and says, 'Uh, um, Mr. Luden, could you explain to me why we're all here and why we exist and why this class is important?' That bacteria answer isn't going to fly, *Doctor*."

"Why is it always a 'her' in the hypothetical scenarios?"

"Just answer the question."

Molly put her head back onto my chest and for a long time I thought about this question of humanity. I thought about why I was here, why Molly and I were together, why we wanted to populate the world with our progeny, and all I knew was that I'd been trying to answer these questions for my entire life.

"I can't just give you an answer," I said. "Philosophers and scientists and preachers and every crazy man on the street has been trying to answer that question since the beginning of time. It's like trying to define love. All I know is that I was put here to love you, to love whatever children we have, to love our life, to make some kind of difference. And maybe I'll succeed and maybe I'll fail, but at least I would have tried, right? Right? Molly?"

It was useless. She was fast asleep.

Now, in the middle of the lake, I think that I should have woken her, should have told her that none of the philosophy mattered. None of the history mattered. All that was important was that we had one another. We could've figured out the rest some other night. In the end, I guess I never told Molly how I felt, and that was my fault. It never hurt to tell the truth, no matter how many times I'd lied.

I was here three weeks ago.

I was here two months ago.

I was here a year ago.

I've never been far enough away from Molly. I've never been close enough to Molly.

I fire the throttle back up and the boat jumps forward.

I am never leaving here.

FOURTEEN

THE TRUTH: I drove to Granite Lake three weeks ago.

I had made the drive several times before, winding through the center of Washington State like a coil, stopping in Ellensburg to think about what I was doing, to consider my options. Once getting as far as Chelan, and then turning around, only to make the same trip the next day.

I'd park my rental car at Morgan's Landing and hike through the woods until I was mere feet from my home. I'd hunker down in the bushes and watch Molly, imagining the cadence of her voice as she talked herself through a painting, smelling her skin on the clothes and towels she hung outside to dry, picking up her litter as I circled the house. And there were times, I will admit, that I found myself staring into the windows of our home very late at night, imagining myself beneath the sheets where Molly slept.

This time, I knew I would not pause along the road, knew I would not merely sit in the woods and watch our cabin from afar. I'd been invited to celebrate our survival, our defeat, our marriage, our losses. It was the anniversary of Katrina's death.

"Don't let Bruce know you're coming," Molly whispered. She was calling from inside Bruce's house. "Just drive around the lake."

"I couldn't get a flight so I'm driving up. I have to come along the backside anyway," I said. "But why does it matter what Bruce thinks?"

"It's confusing," she said. "I don't think he'd approve of you coming out here after all that has happened."

"I don't much care about his opinion."

"No," she said, "I don't suppose you would. But I have to live here, Paul. That means I have to make concessions."

"You don't have to live there. You could come back to me." I believed then as I believe now: that our chances to be together were not predicated on any primitive idea of time, that we'd have eternity to work out the beginning and the end of our relationship. That all the tiny, meaningless, hurtful things we'd said to each other over the years could be smoothed over like marble, until all the rough edges of our life were stains beneath the surface.

"Paul," she said, her voice still just a whisper, "my life has changed for the better without you. I'm sorry if that hurts your feelings, but I feel I should be honest."

"Yes," I said, and it was as though time had melted in my hand. "I understand how that could happen. I won't say anything to anyone about coming there, if that makes you feel better. I'll put it away in a box and hide it under my bed."

"That's fine," she said, though I hoped I would hear her laugh. It had been so long since I'd heard her unrestrained.

"When you get here, we'll figure it all out, right? We'll get everything sorted out and it will be a happy day for both of us."

"I hope so," I said.

"It will be, Paul," she said and then, almost as an after thought, "and we'll be together and that will be happy, too. It will be our own personal day of atonement."

"I believe that," I said, but she'd already hung up.

We'd made promises to each other before and had seemingly come up short each time. But, and I knew this with certainty, this would be different. We'd promised to get through our lives without each other, without our daughter, and we'd succeeded in some way, had managed to live and breathe and we we're going to keep on.

I reached the lake at just past eight o'clock on the anniversary of my daughter's death and for a long time I just drove, not hoping to see anything or feel anything, but to remember what it was like to be *normal*, to not have celebrations about terrible things. I parked my rented Taurus a half-mile from our house almost from habit and walked through the trees and the shrubs, listening to the forest. And what I remembered about being normal was that I would never have done what I was doing. I'd be in bed; my body curled against Molly's, my baby asleep in the other room. My biggest concerns would be the lesson plan for my class, the grocery list, the oil change my car needed.

Before I went back to the car, I made a pact with myself that I would never come back to this lake, would stop forcing myself to live in a state of suspended sorrow for a child I couldn't save and a wife I never wanted to lose. I would learn to love Ginny as I knew she had begun to love me.

But now, as I slow Bruce Duper's boat to a crawl a hundred yards from our dock, I understand that I was being foolish, that I was sick, that I am sick, that the only assurances I could make then was that my life had been unpredictable and would continue to be so. I'd made promises that I could never keep, again.

I cut the engine and the boat coasts quietly into the slip, cutting through the water like a whisper, a memory, a shadow. I tie her in and jump out. Our old Whaler is sitting just as I found it, the Johnson engine shiny and new.

Of course it wasn't a locksmith.

Molly probably mentioned to Bruce that the front door kept blowing open, that the latch was old and rusted, and couldn't he help her out? Couldn't he come out one afternoon and take a look at it?

Of course he could.

Molly didn't love Bruce Duper, couldn't have found him attractive, couldn't have needed him for anything but convenience.

I'm not thinking straight.

She told me. She told me everything.

"Do you remember the day we bought this pile of junk?" I asked. I was standing on the dock, where I am now, staring at the boat, remembering our life on it. The boat had been waxed and the Evinrude looked clean. "How do you keep it running? I mean; I just don't see you crawling around the engine. Do you have somebody who takes care of the old girl?"

"Paul," she said, "let's not do this now. It's late and we're both tired and this isn't how I want to start everything out."

"Then answer the question."

She sighed and then a shiver went through her. "It's Bruce, okay? Does that make you happy? Does that satisfy you?"

"Why would he wax your boat?" I said. "Why would a friend do something like that? Friends don't do things like that, Molly. Let's get real."

"Please, Paul," she said.

"Do you love him, is that it?" Molly started walking back up to the house. "I'm talking to you," I said. Molly stopped and then just grinned at me, as if I'd said something funny.

"Why did you even come here?"

"For Katrina," I said.

"Then let's not argue about a boat, okay?" She was still grinning. I wanted to run down the length of the dock and sweep her into my arms, place kisses over her mouth, her neck, down her chest and stomach. I wanted to dissolve into her, until we were one person.

"Yes," I said. "I'm sorry."

I GO AROUND back and enter the cabin through the kitchen again, just as I did when Ginny and I first got here a few days ago. The kitchen is clean now and I see that Ginny has scrubbed the sink, mopped the floors, placed fresh flowers in the vase on the table. Stress causes Ginny to clean. When we first began dating, when she was afraid I would be fired for seeing her, when her parents were threatening to cut her off, Ginny came to my apartment and scoured every wall, vacuumed every floor, washed every article of my clothing.

I sit down at the table and I try to concentrate, try to remember the tricks Dr. Loomis taught me back when I was a child. He told me to focus on the things that troubled me. He told me to break them down into tiny fragments, small enough to fit on the head of the pin, he said, and then separate them. "Imagine your fears are particles of dust," he said. "Pinpoint each one individually and narrow your mind onto that minuscule piece. And then, Paul, then you can examine it. It is so small it cannot hurt you."

I'm trying to reorder things. I'm trying to focus on myself, on my past without getting trampled up into it. I'm trying not to be afraid.

We are sitting at the kitchen table. It is still dark outside. Molly says to me, "Do you really believe that these were other children?"

"I do."

"And they are ours?"

"Of course."

"But how?"

"Creation is an exact science," I say. "It was meant to be. It was our destiny. These are our two others, Molly."

"I can't believe that," she says.

No. That isn't how it happened. Molly never talked like that. It happened like this: I sat down at the kitchen table while Molly filled a kettle with water to boil for tea. I hadn't been inside our home for over a year, hadn't been this close to Molly for even longer.

"How often do you think of her?" Molly said. She was standing in front of the stovetop watching the blue flames beneath the kettle.

"Every day," I said.

"Is that true?"

"Yes," I said. "She possesses me, Molly. I don't think I can keep living this over and over again."

"Are you seeing a doctor?"

"Yes," I lied.

Molly nodded her head and then closed her eyes. "That's not true, is it?"

"It is true," I said.

"I'm seeing someone now," she said. "It's helped, Paul. It really has. I mean, beyond medication and just talking, it's really made me understand why we didn't work out and why we felt the need to let Katrina fight for herself."

"That's good for you," I said.

"You have to learn to put your trust in something else, that's all." She smiled at me. "I'm wondering how it is that you got here tonight. How we got here tonight. Do you feel guilty, Paul?"

"I want to," I said, and that was the truth. "Sometimes it's almost like it never happened. Like I was never here."

"You can't just keep blacking things out," Molly said. "I found that out. Painting has helped. Do you have a hobby, Paul? Do you have anything besides yourself?"

"I'm dating a girl," I said. "She's young. Nineteen. It's dumb. She's just a replacement."

"For me or for Katrina?" Molly wasn't looking at me anymore. She'd gone to the pantry and was rifling through it, as though we weren't even speaking. There was no emotion in her. I thought perhaps she'd finally figured out how to disconnect herself. "I guess that's not fair to ask," she said. "Forget I said anything. Let's just concentrate on the future. I haven't forgotten anything, couldn't if I wanted to. But I'm only interested in the future now. After this weekend it's all about tomorrow. Don't you think that's the best?"

"We did a horrible thing, Molly," I said. "That's the thing I keep coming back to. We could have saved her if we'd really tried. Do you know what I think? I think I deserve to die for what I've done. All the children we've let die, all the chances we had to make a difference and all we're left with is . . . carcasses. Shells. Just tissue. I never made a difference."

Molly suddenly turned and looked at the back door, as if she thought someone was trying to burst through it, or that someone was going to come and knock on it, rescue her from this moment. But there was no one out there, of course, and Molly quickly turned back to me. Her face was pale.

"I feel like I'm coming down with something," she said.

"Molly," I said.

"I get a pain in my ears," she said. "It feels like something is trying to wiggle out. Have you ever gotten that? It's nothing, I'm sure."

"I brought the pictures back with me," I said. "I want you to see them. I want you to understand what I'm talking about. I've studied them. Those tumors were *children*, Molly. Do you understand that?"

"I'm not hearing you," she said. "It makes no sense."

"I'll show you," I said. "We'll sketch them out. And I'll take them back with me to Los Angeles and I'll submit them to a journal or a magazine or to a university. We can help other people with this."

Molly said then, very calmly, "They're going to arrest us, Paul. Eventually we'll be arrested for letting her die out here.

Some new sheriff will take over, will see what we did, and we'll go to jail."

"I still love you," I said. "Do you know that?"

"You shouldn't," Molly said. "That's what I know. And I also know that we've both had lapses—maybe you don't see it like I do now, but that's what I think they were—lapses. Because we were normal for a while, weren't we? Didn't we have picnics and didn't we make love and didn't we celebrate holidays? We did, didn't we?"

"I'm not sure it matters," I said.

"Do you ever wonder when it's all going to run up behind us? When the avalanche is going to catch us?" Molly sat down across from me and for a moment I thought I might just get up and leave, that coming back again, seeing Molly again, was a mistake. But then she took my hands in hers and held them, stroking my wrist. "How did I get so sick? Tell me, Paul, how did I stop caring about our baby?"

"It's a disease," I said. "You couldn't control it."

"That's not right," she said. "We went crazy. We did. But from what? I can't even look at my paintings from then. It's like I was another person entirely."

"You were," I said. "We were."

"I guess I would like to see the pictures again," she said. "It's so clinical, though. There's not even a piece of her left in them. It won't hurt me to see them, will it?"

"No," I said.

"Okay," she said. "Just get them, then."

Before I'd even reached the guest room, where my bags were, where the autopsy photos were, I could already hear Molly crying.

THERE IS A place inside my head that holds all of my memories about Katrina, about Molly, and about the last month. It has closed itself, it seems, to protect me. I knew before I left for Granite Lake that I needed to lie to Ginny about where I was going. Or, rather, wasn't going.

The day before I left, I told her that I needed to grade papers all weekend, that I'd probably just sit in my apartment with the stereo on reading my work. I told her to call me and we could talk, but that I knew I wouldn't be able to go out. She was fine with everything.

"We'll go out next weekend," Ginny said. "Maybe we can go to a nice dinner in Hollywood at some place where I can see some stars."

"Sure," I said.

"And besides," she said, "I really need to be working on my screenplay this weekend anyway."

Before I left town, I had all my calls forwarded to my cell phone. Ginny would never know where I was.

Now, I think about what I must have known was going to happen.

I run my hands over the kitchen table and imagine that Molly is sitting across from me again. Would I do the same things? Would I say the same words? Even though so much time had elapsed since Katrina died, and even though Molly seemed well, or better at least, I should have known that I was her enabler, that I was the spark that always ignited her.

"Damn it," I say and am surprised by my voice.

I close my eyes and Molly is there. I can smell her. I can taste her lips. She is beside me, she is in front of me, she is inside me. I reach out to touch her. Her voice says, "You saved me."

I've never saved anything, I say.

It's true, her voice says, if you hadn't come here, I might never have had the courage.

You always had courage, I say.

You gave it to me, her voice says. I know you used to come out here and watch me. I know you've seen things that you regret seeing, but none of that matters now. We've come to a very important place in our relationship. You caught the avalanche, Paul.

I listen to Molly telling me the truth. When I open my eyes, the sun has begun to peek through the blinds. It is five eleven in the morning. I've been asleep, dreaming of a ghost.

THE TRUTH: CASES of *fetus in fetu* are terribly rare. The oldest noted cases are often described as a replication of the birth of Eve from the rib of Adam. Yet, a baby boy born in England in the sixteenth century with a tumor consisting of an eye, molar teeth, and fragments of bone was burned in a public square and condemned as the work of the devil. His mother was stoned to death. In 1974, at a dig in Pakistan, anthropologists unearthed a series of near complete Neanderthal fossils. In the pelvic sac of the smallest male were the remains of a tumor roughly a quarter the size of a human fist. It contained what was determined to be two small fingers and the ball-and-socket joint of a shoulder.

The first tumors doctors found in Katrina were small and contained amounts of what they considered nonlethal fluids and substances. "They are simple anomalies," the first doctor said. His name was Vasquez. "Dermoid cysts are, at most, troublesome, often painful, but they can be removed and rarely return. Really, Mr. Luden, the care you give your child is no different because of these. Katrina is very special and these cysts will probably stop occurring by the time she is three."

So we brought her home, back to the lake, and she grew like any child, and once every three weeks I brought her back to the doctor. And once every three weeks Dr. Vasquez said, "This should really stop occurring. That said, it is strictly an annoyance. If you would like, we can keep her here for observation."

"No," I said. "She's just a baby."

"Exactly," he said. "Nothing to be concerned with."

Katrina never cried much, and I think that is a testament to her strength. She wanted to live; I know that. Even when the tumors started attacking her brain, she acted no differently. But that isn't so odd. Brain tumors can be the most pleasant of all killers, the victims rarely knowing that they are dying until they are dead.

Finally, three months before she died, the doctors in Granite City called in a specialist from Seattle. His name was Dr. Sigal. He was tall and thin and fiddled with a pen as he spoke to us. We were sitting in the waiting room at the Granite City clinic with Katrina asleep across Molly's lap.

"It is difficult for me to explain this to you," Dr. Sigal said, "because I've never dealt extensively with this sort of thing in a child. I believe the recurring tumors in your daughter's abdomen are teratomas, not malignant mind you, but of an odd makeup. They don't seem to be made of the typical masses, yet exhibit many of the same properties."

"What are you saying?" Molly said.

"I think your daughter is dying," he said flatly. "She's being eaten from the inside by these tumors. They're sucking protein from her and diverting oxygen. It is the most unbelievable thing I've ever seen. It deserves proper study."

"She's not a guinea pig," I said.

"She is remarkable," Dr. Sigal said. "Katrina should never have survived childbirth. Science needs her, Mr. Luden, you must understand that."

"I want to go home," Molly said.

"The only thing I know is that my child is not going to be hooked up to a bunch of machines," I said.

"It's her best chance," Dr. Sigal said.

"I think I'm coming down with something," Molly said.

"What percentage do you give her, Doctor? Five? Ten?" I paused as Katrina stretched one arm out, swallowed, and then turned on her side. "Can you quantify the chance my daughter has to live versus your chance to get into a textbook?"

"You don't know the first thing about science," Dr. Sigal said. "This is a landmark. I'll do everything in my power to secure your daughter the finest physicians. We can make her very comfortable. And of course you'd be compensated."

I'd spent so many hours in hospital waiting rooms determining the fate of my children. I'd spent years of my life talking to doctors who swore they could fix everything: Dr. Loomis, Dr. Plinkton, and now Dr. Sigal. I wanted to grab Katrina and sprint out of the office, run down the highway, run all the way to the coast and dive into the Pacific. We could swim with the outgoing tide, our bodies lifted along the crest of the waves, floating and floating, the sun bright and shining and we would be gone from here and we would be home, finally, home.

"I'm taking my family home," I said.

"She won't live without medical attention," Dr. Sigal said.

"She won't live with it," I said.

Dr. Sigal started to say something then paused. There was nothing he could say.

We took Katrina home and Molly put her down on the bed in our bedroom; where I am sitting now. I'm holding the manila envelope filled with my daughter. I open the clasp and pull out two glossy eight-by-tens of the tumor the doctors found in Katrina's brain.

I want to close my eyes again, so that I can hear Molly, but instead I just focus on the tumors, remembering, modifying, visualizing.

I'd walked into the guestroom, where my bags were, and gathered up all of the documents relating to Katrina's death, the photos, the diagrams, the theories, what amounted to the truth. The pathologists in Granite City had provided me with the pictures they took of Katrina and the results of the tests they'd done of her. The autopsy stated that Katrina "a two-year-old female, died as a result of a tumor on the base of her medulla oblongata." Signed, sealed, delivered, Katrina's life summed up in one sentence. I'd collected hundreds of pages of documents relating to the masses found in my daughter, had completed complex diagrams that outlined the process by which the tumors were diverting proteins, had outlined several areas of study regarding the historical and anthropological significance of our daughter.

I'd broken Katrina down into a science. I knew her every pore. I knew the probability within 1.7 percent of a child born to two manic-depressives to suffer physiological or psychological abnormalities. Molly and I were going to finally get down to the science of our child's death. We were going to celebrate what I'd always known: That nothing could save her from life. We'd enabled a disaster.

I walked down the hallway back toward the kitchen with the papers in my hands, prepared to deal with Molly's sinking psyche. Prepared to leave our home forever and start living life. But with every breath another memory cascaded back to me, as they do now, buffeted by emotions I'd held back, so that it seemed like every second was a year of my life. I concentrated on what I knew was true: Molly and I were as dead as our daughter, our chances of being anything more to each other save for painful memories was over. These drawings, these pictures—the clinical dispersion of all my dead children—were useless. The instant they were made, the very moment I drew them, their quantification stopped mattering. I turned around and went back to the guest room and stuffed the pictures beneath the bed, figuring I would tell Molly that I'd lost them, had forgotten them, and had decided that the life of our child, while fragile, didn't need to be understood. It was what it was.

There was a knock at the door. I heard Molly get up from the table and walk to the front door.

"Bruce," Molly said. "I told you not to come tonight."

"I had to see you," he said.

"It's almost midnight," Molly said.

"Is he here?" Bruce said. "I know he's here."

"Go home," Molly said. "None of this concerns you."

"You concern me," he said.

"I want you out of my home, Bruce," Molly said.

I stood there in the hallway and listened to silence. I thought I could hear Bruce Duper breathing, panting, preparing to charge.

"Are you going to be okay with him here?" Bruce said finally.

"I'm by myself," she said. "And I'm fine."

"You look like you've been crying," he said.

"I'm coming down with something," she said. "I'm just very tired."

"Maybe you've just decided to give me up," Bruce said. "Maybe that's it?"

"It's late," Molly said.

"My attitude about this has changed," Bruce said. He sounded whimsical, almost. Like he'd read a book about how to fall into and out of love. "You know, it was kinda hazy at first, dreamlike. I felt like things were really happening between you and me. I was always excited. Have you ever felt like that?"

"Of course," Molly said softly.

"Both of us miserable," he said.

"You've been drinking," Molly said.

"Does it even matter?" Bruce said. "You know how I've felt about you for over a year. That's a big chunk of both of our lives. Here I am, drunk on the porch. Why do you think men do such stupid things? This isn't the way to make you happy, is it?" I stepped around the corner into the kitchen and peeked out into the living room. Bruce was standing in the doorframe. He had on a pair of blue jeans and a flannel shirt. He'd tugged a baseball cap over his ears, the bill just above his eyes, and it made his head look shrunken. "Anyway, I guess this doesn't have to be the end. I can just keep on doing what I'm doing. Right, Molly?"

"I want you to leave," she said.

"My judgment's all messed up," Bruce said. "I'm awful sorry about all of this." He rocked back on his heels and I heard him sigh. He looked lost, like everything he'd ever wanted had just trickled between his fingers. "I can call the sheriff if you want me to. He knows Paul's been creeping around here off and on."

"He's not here," Molly said.

"I guess that car parked out back is someone else's," Bruce said, and then both of them were quiet again. I thought I should just walk into the living room and say hello, shake hands with Bruce, thank him for being kind to my wife in my absence. "I'm sorry, Molly, I really am. I've been drinking all night like some dumb kid. I'll probably drown on my way back. I'm just not together on this. You've turned me inside out."

Molly exhaled audibly. "Just stay here for a minute, okay?" she said. "Don't go anywhere." When she closed the door, I stepped out of the kitchen.

"I'll go," I said.

"No," she whispered. "He's drunk. I'm just going to put him to bed. He's in no condition to go back across the lake."

"What do you want me to do?"

Molly nibbled on her thumbnail for a moment. It reminded me of the moment I first knew I loved her; back in her dorm room, on the floor, her hair in a ponytail. So beautiful. So precious.

"Paul, what's wrong," Molly said. She had her hand on my arm. "Open your eyes."

"Sorry," I said. "I was just concentrating."

"Go out back," she said. "Just wait out back for a few minutes. Let me put Bruce into bed."

"Does he love you?" I asked. We were standing at the back door.

"It's not always about love," Molly said. "Why is it always about love with you? Can't he just *hurt*?" She was whispering, but I could tell that Molly wanted to scream. "I'm sorry about it. I'm sorry he's here. It's my fault. He feels very strongly about me. He cares about me. I'm just not ready for that kind of thing."

"Then he does," I said. Molly put her head down and just shook it, though I could tell she wasn't really mad. Just frustrated and sad. "I'll wait then. Let me know when I can come back inside."

I stood there in the dark and paced. It felt like everything was at stake; that my life had changed perceptibly in the last fifteen minutes. So Bruce Duper was in love with my wife? What was the difference? Ginny loved me and I had already determined that I was going to try to reciprocate. The difference was that Bruce didn't understand the depth of our relationship, couldn't possibly understand that life and death had forgotten how to act when Molly and I were together. Bruce didn't know that I'd already been opened up wide and that my world had a tendency to hang on a tipping axis. He didn't know that I thought that I was finally seeing things clearly. That I was turning a corner.

He didn't know that I'd stopped taking my medication and that I was standing outside breaking down the words he spoke to my wife into symbols, cutting rough edges off of some letters, turning others over in my mind, flipping sounds around until they were unintelligible, until there was nothing left; until Bruce Duper failed to exist to me.

FIFTEEN

MY MOTHER TOLD me before she died that she thought I had turned out all right, that I'd been a troubling boy but had turned into a loving husband, a good father. "And a good son," she said. I was sitting next to her on a couch in the living room of my childhood home in Walnut Creek. Dad had brought her home the day before, after it had become pointless to keep her in the hospital.

"I'm sorry if I caused you grief," I said.

"There's not a worry in me anymore," she said. A hospice nurse was lingering nearby, watching the levels of morphine in the IV drip she'd hooked up to my mom. She caught my eye and smiled wanly. I thought then what a great sacrifice one must make to choose death as a means of living. To be a nurse, or a doctor, or an anthropologist, you must decide early on that you are working toward a greater good.

"I know I scared you," I said. "I never meant to."

"I'm still willing to try," she said. I looked up again and the nurse was staring at me.

"It's the morphine," the nurse said. "Just keep talking to her."

"Sunday mornings were the best," Mom said suddenly, though her eyes were closed. "That was real family time, wasn't it? We had fun sometimes."

"Always," I said.

"Your father wanted to abort you," she said. "We'd failed so many times, he didn't want to go through that again. I didn't blame him. But it was illegal."

My dad was in the kitchen with Molly, playing with Katrina.

"You just rest now, Mrs. Luden," the nurse said.

Mom stopped talking then, as if on cue. Her chest was heaving but no air seemed to be coming into or out of her.

"Is she okay?" I said.

The nurse adjusted the pillows beneath my mother's head and fixed her blankets before answering me. "No," she said. "I'm afraid not."

"How much of that morphine can she take?"

"As much as she'd like," the nurse said. She was an older black woman with a tight wrinkled quality to her skin, as though she'd been stretched to the point of breaking, and then released. "It has a disorienting effect. Not everything she says will make perfect sense."

"Don't worry," I said. "I'm a big boy."

The nurse sat down on a folding chair we'd brought in from the garage and picked up a magazine from the coffee table but didn't open it.

"What do you do?" she said.

"I'm a teacher," I said.

"That's a good job," she said.

"When do you think she'll die?"

The nurse looked at my mother kindly, like this was the toughest thing she'd ever witnessed. "Hard to say," she said. "Never can tell when a person is ready to go. Sometimes they hold out to see a relative or to tell someone something. Folks got a lot of claim over their souls, I think. Your mom seems strong. Maybe a week?"

"You really believe that?" I said. "About the souls?"

"I've seen some things in this job," she said, and I believed her. If you spend enough time around sick people, I found out much later on, the most unbelievable things become just like real life.

"Do you think everyone has a soul?" I said. "There's some awful people in this world."

"I believe everyone is human," she said. "No boogie men, if you know what I'm saying. That's what separates you and me and your mom here from, say, a dog or monkey. We got *spirit*. So if you're a murderer or, say, a nurse like me, God got a place for you. Don't mean it has to be a nice place."

My mom opened her eyes then and coughed hard. "You all right, miss?" the nurse said.

"I'd like some water," my mom said and then went right back to sleep.

"She's got a lot of spirit," the nurse said.

"What about me?"

"You're a mixed bag," she said and laughed. So did I. "Oh, this is a trying time. You'll be all right. You got a family. That always helps. I guess you've known your mother was gonna pass for some time now, anyway. That helps prepare you. But once it comes down for real, when it's upon you like this here, it gets kinda mealy. Can't let it consume you, I'd say. But you seem like you know that."

"I guess then I do," I said after a while. "A week, then. Seven whole days and nights."

"Twenty-four hours in each of them," she said. She'd opened up the magazine on her lap and was flipping absently through the pages, not really reading anything.

My mother died that night. We sat around her body for a long time, not talking or crying or calling anybody on the phone. The nurse had left us alone to call the proper authorities and then had just stayed in the kitchen.

"She looks peaceful, doesn't she?" my dad said.

"She does," I said.

"Like she can finally sleep."

"It's been a long time since she's had a decent rest," I said.

"I wish Katrina had gotten a chance to know her," Dad said to Molly. "It's good to have grandparents."

"We'll tell Katrina all about her," Molly said. Dad leaned over and patted Molly's foot. It was one of the only times I ever saw him touch her.

"I'll say this," Dad said. "You never knew her like I did, Paul. It's a shame. She was a hard woman to understand, had some strange ideas and such, but she loved you dearly. Worried about you constantly."

"I know that," I said and then we were all silent again until there was a knock on the door and the nurse let in two men from the funeral home.

"You'll fix her up, right?" Dad said to the men. "You'll make her look beautiful again?"

"Of course, sir," one of them said.

"I'd like to kiss her," Dad said to no one in particular and then did, slowly, on her lips and forehead and then he took her hands and rubbed them along his cheek.

AFTER THEY CAME and took my mother that night, I sat on the front porch with my father and watched him smoke a cigar. It was late, near midnight, and a spectral fog had rolled in, giving everything a soft, gloomy edge.

"Mom said you wanted me aborted," I said. "Is that true?"

Dad sucked on his cigar until the tip glowed red and then exhaled slowly. "It was a different time. We'd had so many problems. I didn't want the disappointment again."

"How close did it come?"

Dad stared into the fog for a time before he answered me. "We tried to get it done, but you were too far along. We drove into Mexico, got all the way into the waiting room of a clinic there before we turned around."

"What changed your mind?"

"She felt you kick," Dad said. "That's all we needed. You were born three months later."

"Did you ever regret not staying?"

Dad blew a stream of smoke through his nose and then stood up and stretched his arms high above his head. He looked old to me, like he might not last another hour. "This is a happy day," he said. "Your mother is at rest and you have your entire life in front of you. Everything is wide open for you now. No lines keeping you tethered anymore. Why not just forget about the bad stuff, Paul? Why let it inhabit your life?"

"I can't get rid of it," I said. "It's who I am now. It's who I've always been."

"That's not true," he said. He sounded at once tired and angry; as if this was a conversation he'd had before and had not liked how it ended. "This is how you've made yourself. You weren't born into despair. The choices you've made stink on you like a dead skunk."

"You didn't answer my question."

"If you knew the trouble we went through just to have you," he said and then just stopped. Molly had walked out onto the porch with Katrina awake in her arms and neither of us had even noticed.

"We were just talking," I said.

"I didn't mean to interrupt," she said.

"It's all right," Dad said. "We were through." He went inside and went to bed.

I'd see my father alive three times after that night, once at the funeral for my mother, once at the funeral for Katrina, and once, oddly, at the airport in Spokane a few days before he, too, died. Katrina had been gone for over a year. I'd flown into Spokane to watch Molly. We passed each other like strangers, both of us stopping a few yards away.

"I didn't see you," he said.

"No," I said. "I didn't see you either."

"This is a surprise," he said. We hadn't spoken since Katrina's funeral.

"Where are you going?" I said.

"I'm on a layover," he said. "I'm flying to Canada. British Columbia."

"It's nice this time of year," I said. He looked worried and at once expectant, as though this moment were filled with possibilities for him. "Are you meeting someone?"

My dad blushed. "Yes," he said. "I met her online. We've been spending a good deal of time together."

"That's good for you," I said. "You're still a young man."

"What are you doing here?"

"Molly and I are going to give it another go," I lied, though I believed that then. "See if we can fix things."

"You owe her that." A plane filled with passengers coming back from Hawaii was disembarking around us. Everyone was wearing floral print shirts, straw hats, flip-flops. My dad was wearing a suit and tie. "People used to know how to dress when they traveled," he said.

"A lot of things have changed," I said.

"Yes," he said. "You look well, though. You look great. Like you are really happy. Are you really happy, Paul?"

"I'm not," I said.

"No," he said. "I suppose you aren't."

Reunited families were hugging each other all around us and I could tell my father felt uncomfortable.

"You must have a plane to catch," I said.

"You should try and become happy, Paul," Dad said. "You've spent your whole life like this. But, you know, you still have time, you can still decide to make something positive out of all of this. That's what I'm doing. I'm living again. It feels good, son, it feels mighty good."

"I'm glad to hear that," I said. "Are you going to marry this woman?"

"Oh, I don't know about that sort of thing," he said. "I still love your mother a great deal. Like you must still love Molly."

"Molly's still here," I said. "I guess the challenge for me is to just make things right." Dad didn't respond. He'd pushed himself onto his tiptoes and was looking out into a crowd of people coming down the concourse.

"She should be here anytime now," he muttered after the group had passed us.

"I'd like to meet her," I said.

Dad grimaced then like he'd been stuck with a cattle prod. "She doesn't know about my old life," he said. "I figured that she wouldn't want to be burdened with the details. It feels good. To her I'm not a widower or the manager of a restaurant. It's like an adventure. I can be whomever I want. You understand that, don't you?"

"I don't," I said.

"I'm happy for the first time in a long time," he said and then he took my hand in his and shook it. "It was good to see you. You look good. You look like you're on your way to becoming happy."

"I am then," I said. My dad's hand was trembling and I got the sense that this was just how he'd wanted this conversation to go, whenever he had it with me. "I'm better in all possible ways."

My dad let go of my hand and patted me once on the back as if we were old friends, our meeting shaped strictly by chance. "You give Molly and Katrina all my love," he said, not catching his slip, and then he just backed away smiling, like I was a distant shadow from a life he'd completely vacated. If I'd known then that he only had a few more days to live, I might have told him that I loved him and that I was sorry I'd made such a mess of things. I might have said that I'd like another chance to grow up with him and Mom, in a different time and under different circumstances.

I remember all of this as I sit and stare at the pictures of Katrina. Time and circumstance have ruled every aspect of my life: I've never made proper use of either. All the times I'd come back here, to this lake, with the intent to say to Molly that we should try to get back with each other, that we should try to have another child, that we should try to get really happy, but all that ever transpired was that I would sit in the woods and watch her life. It was as though I was hunting her existence, letting her stray only a few precious feet from me sometimes, so close that I could smell her perfume, so close that I could touch her, could pet the loose strands of her hair, could blow kisses onto her cheek.

It was in those times that I got the sense again that there wasn't a clear line inside me, that I'd somehow overlapped— that the part of me that was human and the part of me that had evolved from animal ceased to exist. I was an anomaly, a trick in evolution. The truth is that I think my dad knew everything he needed to know about me that day in the airport.

I was forgettable.

When Molly asked me to go outside that night, I did willingly. I stood in the shadows for over an hour, paced around the trees, thought about life and love. Thought about my daughter. I decided then that I wasn't a horrible person. That if given the chance, I think I'd like to meet me, would like to share a cup of coffee with me, would have a nice time finding out about how I lived. Sure, I'd let my lines go slack now and again, had done some things that were crazy, had made mistakes with the people who I loved, but I thought that this night was something of a turning point: I was hiding outside so my wife could put a man who loved her to bed.

"I'm sorry," she said, stepping out onto the back porch. She had my overnight bag in her hand. "I wanted this night to go differently."

"I'm fine," I said, and I think now that I must have believed that. Must have thought that this wasn't the kind of thing I'd obsess over. I was wrong.

"He's drinking again," Molly said.

"I didn't know he had a problem."

"Yes you do," Molly said. "Remember the night we saw him at the Branding Iron?"

"No," I said, but then I heard Kenny Rogers singing in my head, heard Molly say that Bruce looked like a real man, but that he was probably no smarter than the fish he caught on the lake, heard her say that the time was now, that an egg was dropping. "Wait. I do remember that."

"Maybe we can do this tomorrow?"

"Yes," I said. "We can do that."

Molly handed me my bag. "Let me go back inside to make sure he's asleep and then I'll walk you back to your car. Okay?"

"You don't have to."

"Please wait." Molly touched me on the arm. "I'll be right back."

SIXTEEN

I SLIDE THE photos of Katrina back into the envelope and walk out the front door. The sun is up and, despite the storm last night, the sky is clear. It looks purple to me, but I know it's just a trick of light. Everything is as it is supposed to be. Nothing has changed in the last twenty-four hours.

What a slow process this life is. We die in sixty-second increments every day. Things cannot continue to slip away forever; at some point all of this must end. And where does that leave me? I'm not ready to leave this world without some sense that I've done what's right at least once. I want to leave a mark, something more than the stain that already exists. The truth: I believe now that Molly is dead.

I believe I may have killed her.

Time has gone missing for me, days and weeks turning to ash in my mind, so that I'm not sure what I've done, what I've seen. I'm not certain that I'm capable of rearranging events correctly anymore.

I turn and look at our house. It seems so small. Hardwood floors and a view of the lake couldn't save me. So many lives lost to such a tiny place.

Each step I take triggers another scene in my mind, so that I wonder if I ever lived here in complete happiness, or if my mind has always opened like a trap door and I've slid through it all, blinded by the speed.

"Why don't you at least come out and get your stuff," Molly said to me once on the phone. I'd been back in L.A. for just over a month. I'd been out of the hospital for two months. They gave me a clean bill of health, prescribed me Paxil, told me to let go, get back to the things I love doing.

"I'm coming back," I said. "We'll be a family. We have a house."

"Are you still on medication?"

"Yes," I said. "For a while."

"That's good," she said.

"I've made some drawings," I said. "I appreciated you coming down to the hospital and showing me how. It will help my research."

"It was just basic," she said.

"I made some drawings of you," I said. "I'd like for you to see them someday."

"Maybe I will."

"I guess what I want to say is that you've helped me," I said. "More than any doctor or psychologist. It was always you who made things seem substantial."

"Let's not do this anymore," she said. "Let's not have every conversation be a 'session.' Can't we just speak like adults?"

"I don't think so," I said.

"No," she said and I thought I heard her laugh. "Too many nights on the ledge, I guess."

"I'm teaching again," I said. "They've hired me at Pierce."

"That's good," she said and then neither of us spoke for a moment. "I want to ask you some things, because it's troubling me. And I guess it contradicts everything I just said. But I need to know. Did you hurt Katrina? I remember you cutting her hair and she was crying. Did that happen?"

"I never hurt her," I said. "She'd never seen her hair come off. She didn't know what was happening."

"Is that true?"

"Yes," I said, and it was, is.

"I remember you holding her, like she was hurt."

"She wasn't," I said. "You know what she did, Molly? She told me that she loved me. It is my fondest memory of her."

"She never said that to me," Molly said.

"I'm sorry for that," I said and for a moment Molly was silent. In my mind, I could see her holding the phone beside her ear, trying to find words where none existed.

"You aren't still reordering things, are you?" she asked.

"No," I said. "I know where everything fits."

"I'll just send you your stuff," she said. "Okay? Is that fine? I'll get Bruce to come out and UPS it all to you."

"It will have to be," I said.

"I want you to stay on your medication."

"I will."

I kneel down and dig my hands into the sand; it feels cool and damp and I think that all of this has been put here just for me. The whole world was built to serve me, the earth, the sun, the moon, all of God's people, placed here to be my lab. And the birds fly just for me. And the wind blows just for me. I've gotten what I've always wanted: I am free now. I am so terribly free.

I stood outside, behind the house, and waited for Molly. I imagined her walking barefoot across the hardwood floor, going into our bedroom and checking on Bruce, leaning over, kissing him on the forehead, sliding into bed beside him.

This is not happening, I thought. My arm felt warm from where she'd touched it. How long had it been since she'd touched me? Years, I thought. Years since her touch was electric on my skin, since I deserved it, years since I'd run through this forest with Katrina in my arms. How long since Molly held me and said that everything would be fine, that everyone was trying to help me?

It had been a long while since we'd talked like people, not patients. What made me think I could come back to this house on this lake and think things could ever change toward the positive?

It felt like a lifetime ago, a moment ago, it felt like a grain of sand frozen in an hourglass.

I took a step toward the house and remembered our first night in it, unpacking our dishes and silverware, remembered the moment I knew we'd never leave this place. I took another step and I was on the porch, opening the door back into the kitchen. Had I really seen Bruce Duper there at the house? Had I really heard Molly and him arguing? Had she really stepped outside and touched me on the arm and told me to wait for her? Didn't she know I'd always waited for her?

Yes.

Our teacups were still on the table, the kettle on the stove, and from the other side of the house I could just make out the sounds of Molly cooing to Bruce, coaxing him to sleep.

THINGS OCCUR TO me differently today, standing on my dock on this perfect fall morning.

For the first time, I feel balanced. I feel calm. I feel that things are happening just as they were destined to occur.

This sense of balance, this understanding of gravity, astonishes me. Because, for a time in my childhood, I believe I was invisible. My parents could perceive me only slightly.

I'd walk through school in a trance, touching only the outlines of a real life, speaking only when I had to, and then
coming home and dissecting everything, anything: words,
telephones, animals. I'd cut into anything I could find, hoping to find a center—equilibrium, significance. It never
worked. I'd get into an argument with my mother just so that
I could diagram the sentences she said. I'd rush to my room
to write her words down from memory, breaking down the
prepositional hitches, commas splices, adverbs, nouns, sub-
jects, predicates, her entire way of dealing with me.

There have been moments in my life when I've ques-
tioned if I was actually *real*. It was in those times when I hurt
myself, clawed at my skin, ripped at my hair, just so that I
might feel some kind of pain, something to let me know that
I was *here* and that I was *now*. I've never thought I was entirely human, never understood how I could be asked to exist when I couldn't figure out how, exactly, we'd all come to
be. I could never find that delicate balance.

If my mother were still alive, I would tell her that she
should have been afraid of me. I would tell her that she
should have me removed, she should take me back to Mexico and get me extracted, let me start again.

The day that forward motion ended for my life was when
Katrina died. I've been living in rewind since then. There's a
tendency in me that says I should have just ended it all then.
Ginny, in many ways, saved me. Maybe I do love her. Maybe
I am capable of giving that to her.

I stood in the kitchen and recalled the day I tried to cure
Katrina, remembered the Sundays when Molly and I made
love for hours, the terrible quiet when Katrina was gone
and there was nothing left for us to say, when I thought love
had died.

Love doesn't die, I decided. I was looking at the teakettle
Molly had been warming up before Bruce arrived. Love can
change into other emotions, can linger like a disease in a
dead animal, until it rises again and attacks and you're left

with the sense that it has always been a part of you, even when you thought it was lost forever.

I picked up the kettle to feel the weight of it, to make sure I was tangible, and caught a glimpse of myself in the shined silver. I brushed the hair away from my face where it was matted with sweat, and I saw this: a good-looking man with an honest face, someone who'd led a decent life, had parents who loved him, a profession he valued, had nobody, had nothing, was utterly and without mistake alone.

It seemed perfectly appropriate; my face was that of a man whose endings and beginnings seemed to be the same. I set the kettle back down and quietly backed out of the house.

Half-way through the shrubs, I heard Molly calling for me from the backyard.

"Paul?"

I stopped in the forest and listened to the way her words hung in the air. She called my name again, this time louder, and the letters fell from the sky and crashed around me. I curled myself around the trunk of a tree and waited for Molly to find me.

She would come for me. She would take me back to the house and show me Bruce. She would say, "I love him," and I would try to understand, because I couldn't be hurt anymore. I couldn't be seen or heard or touched or cheated or lied to or told that my daughter was dead or that my wife was loved by another person or that everything, everything, had fallen to pieces.

I stayed in that one spot for a stretch of time that seems endless now. I slept or passed out, because one moment it was dark and in the next the sun was beating down on me and mosquitoes were feasting on my flesh. Time had shuttered itself again.

SEVENTEEN

I HAVE COME to believe that fate is a stronger science than medicine or anthropology. There are so many equations that must be solved before one can understand what fate brings.

There were fifteen thousand other women with me in college, each imbued with a sense of cause and hope that these years spent in university life would lead them to their destiny, that they would find a willful career, a livelihood, and perhaps someone who wanted to share in this life, someone who would complete the symmetry of their existence.

I am haunted by the false equations, by the fateful errors that have brought me back to this lake, beyond a life with the person I'd always loved, to where I am now, questioning my own mind and very best intentions.

Bruce Duper is crossing the lake in his father's old Fischer, his arms waving wildly to attract my attention.

I am standing on the dock on the threshold of a life I'm not sure I've led, trying to piece together the traumas that have caused me to forget who I am and what I've done. A fish jumps and for a moment it seems suspended above the lake, its skin like quicksilver, and then it is gone. I think about Molly and see her as if she were a dream, gliding above the ground, her hair flowing behind her, hands outstretched. I think about how I used to pick her up in my arms and twirl her until she giggled and laughed and begged me to stop, covered my face in kisses. We were so in love then. She was light, peaceful. And then in the kitchen that night three weeks ago—like she'd lost all sense of space and was living in a dead world where there was no reason, no rules. But that was not the truth. The truth was that I'd killed her years before. That night in the kitchen, though, she looked worn down, as if the world had spun much too close to her again, and that, finally, she wanted to push the future forward and end this era of destruction and death earmarked by my arrival.

A Chinook wind has picked up from the north causing the lake to ripple with curled waves. The glare from the sun makes everything seem to be on fire. When I close my eyes, they burn orange, then blue, and Molly is rising from the flames, sailing towards me, Katrina in her arms.

I've never felt so alive.

Bruce shouts, honks the horn on his father's boat. I lift a hand up to let him know that I see him, that I feel him, that he has entered my being like a virus, has infected my capacity to remember things as they actually occurred.

I STOOD UP in the forest and got my bearings. The house was just over a hundred yards away. Either I had run in a circle or I had never left at all. From behind the trees, I could hear voices: a man and a woman.

I prowled the perimeter of my home like a panther, stooping through the trees, sniffing into the air, pausing at any noise. Stepping into the clearing behind the house, I coiled, prepared myself to attack, to launch myself toward whatever it was that I found. I would rip the world to shreds.

She was pacing in the backyard, walking in concentric circles, following the same pattern over and over again, her feet falling in her footsteps. I stood still and imagined myself an animal, camouflaged by my colors, hidden in plain sight.

"Come back inside," he said.

I flinched when I heard his voice, soft and measured, comfortable in my home, in my bed with my wife.

"I don't want to fight about this anymore," Molly said, though she said it to herself.

"Molly," he said, stepping out onto the porch. I wilted back into the trees. "I want to talk about putting an end to this." He waved a handful of papers in the air. "We need to be rid of him, once and for all. Rid of these letters, these drawings, everything."

"Don't tell me what we need to do," she said.

"When I get back home," Bruce said, "I'm calling the sheriff, have him arrest Paul for stalking you. He's a threat, you know. He's not right in the head."

Molly looked up from the ground then and I think she may have sensed me, may have known I was standing only a few feet away. Though our worlds had come to a point that seemed hopeless, she could salvage a portion of herself. She stopped pacing and walked over to Bruce, standing on the porch.

"He'll never be out of our lives," she said. "You'll have to accept that." Molly slid an arm around Bruce's neck and pulled him toward her. Yes, I thought, grab him by the throat and push him away.

No.

They kissed and he held her and she buried her face in his chest, and then he saw me. He called my name and he chased after me. I could feel his footfalls as he lumbered toward me.

No.

I am remembering another day, another man.

Bruce's boat is only twenty feet from the dock now. He is wearing a flannel shirt and jeans and his face is red from the wind whipping against it. "Don't move, Paul. I want to talk to you."

"I'm not mad at you," I say.

He didn't see me there in the woods. What he saw was Molly and he held her and they kissed, and maybe for Bruce life had finally begun. Maybe he'd found the one thing that he'd always wanted—a purpose to wake up each morning, knowing there was another person, another life that depended on him.

I thought that I could never unsee this. I would never wake up and not know that I'd lived this moment. I wished then that I were just an animal, that I could sniff the scent of Bruce and Molly, could run my paw over the matted earth below me, leaving a mark for them to know that I was close, that I could seize upon them if they came too near, and then simply leave without any sense of sovereignty. And I think I even prayed for a moment, which I never do, and asked God to save me, to make me invisible, to let me go on living in some other form.

He lifted her into his arms and I slouched back another ten yards into the forest.

"I love you," he said.

Twenty yards.

"I'll do anything to keep you," he said. "You know that."

Thirty yards.

"I want him gone," he said. "I want you to cut him out forever."

Fifty yards, and I'm sprinting away from this vision, away from this truth, jagged branches stabbing at my face, my ears, my arms, and I'm running for my life, and I'm running with Katrina again, back through the woods, back through time, back to where this all started. I'm holding Katrina in my arms and Sheriff Drew is behind me.

"It's gonna be all right, Paul," he said. "You couldn't save her."

"I have time," I said. "I can put her back."

"She was sick," he said. "I'm real sorry, son, but she's dead. She's dead and you can't bring her back."

"What do you know about what I can do?"

"You're not thinking right," he said. "Your daughter should have been in the hospital. I know that. I know that. Now c'mon, stop running. I'm an old man."

Sheriff Drew was smiling, I remember him smiling, trying to calm me down. I remember looking down at Katrina and thinking that I was a murderer, that she could have been saved, and I deserved to die.

Jumping over fallen trees, stumbling over rocks, heading for the water, for right here, circling back around Sheriff Drew. "Don't," he shouted. Diving into the water with Katrina in my arms, going back to where it all started, back to the bottom of the lake, back to the beginning, giving myself back to earth, starting again, all over, never thinking about life without her and Molly, knowing we'd all be together this way forever, for a life without words, and illness, and abortions and tumors. Together.

BRUCE DUPER STEPS onto the dock and I am reminded that it took us millions of years to learn how to lie, that words have come a long way from the caves of Taung, the open plateaus of Sterkfontein, and the deep gorges of Tanzania.

"You took my boat," he says.

"I'm sorry about that," I says. "I needed to come back."

Bruce sniffles once and then stretches his arms out, like we are meeting casually on a city street after a long day of work. "I called the sheriff," he says.

"Good," I say.

"How do these things happen?" he asks. "How do people forget what they've done?"

"It's an illness," I say. "Did Molly tell you about it?"

"I read some of your letters." Bruce says. "I won't lie. She filled me in on the important things, matters of safety and such."

The real danger now is fear. I believe in science, in formulas, in the delineation of man and beast. I understand the process by which I was created; by which man went from a single cell to this creature I see reflected back to me from the water beside me. I have lived my life with the understanding that it was the only life I would get. Now, today, this very moment, I think about my children, about my wife, about my mom and dad, and I think about Ginny and Leo, and about Bruce Duper standing in front of me here—the people who have loved me, have known parts of me intimately—and I think it is plausible that all my science is wrong. I've made a tragic mistake believing I was put on this earth to understand man.

I've never believed in the Bible or in the Koran or the Torah, but I still think that I can be saved. There is a power in me that says I am my own god, my own dominion, and that only I can determine what comes after all of this has turned to vapor.

"You were there," I say. "I saw you holding her."

"And then what happened?"

"And then," I begin to say, but there is nothing, no words, only a sense of motion: running through the woods, away from the house and then, somehow, back in Los Angeles, in my apartment, grading papers, calling Ginny, living, breathing, taking a phone call that says my wife is missing, a blank spot in time.

"I found your footprints in the dirt," Bruce says.

"I'd been there," I say. "For the anniversary. I'd come up to commemorate Katrina. You showed up drunk and I left."

"I didn't see you," he says.

No, I think, you couldn't have. I've been invisible my entire life. A siren rings out and both of us turn to look.

Cutting across the water is a boat with a twirling blue light. It is more than half a mile away, near the center of the lake, and though I can't see any people aboard, I know who is coming. I look up into the sky and mark the time. It is not yet noon.

"I was hiding," I say.

The siren grows louder. I break it down by pitch, by tone, until it is nothing but a buzz, a jumble of consonants and I think that everything falls apart for a reason. There is no final conclusion to life, nothing to sum up the quality of existence. I wondered for a long time after Katrina died if I would ever see the world as my father once had, rife with chance and hope. I would never get used to parting with things, never get used to saying that I once had a daughter, never get used to feeling like my head was full of soot and that everything had burned around me. In parts of my mind it is obvious to me that the world has never changed, that things have stayed the same, frozen in place for me, frozen in this kind of madness that makes me believe I am a monster, and have done things normal people would shudder at.

The lives that were extinguished around me did not just peter out as one might expect. They smoldered inside me, flared up time and again, searing the terrain.

My body feels tight, like I've been squeezed into a tiny box, and that my ribs will splinter from my chest if I breathe too deeply. I close my eyes and concentrate on being small, on shrinking down to the head of a pin, on making this entire world a white dot.

"Paul," Bruce says, "I want you to calm down."

"I'm fine," I say, because I can now remember waking up in my car, my body cramped with hunger and thirst, only to find myself beneath a tree in a gas station parking lot in Sacramento, hundreds of miles away from Granite Lake.

Think, Molly says in my mind. *Remember.*

Sweet angel, I think. What have I done to you?

I am right here, she says. *I have always been right here.*

I am a meticulous man. I am bound by theories, by carbon, by givens and proofs. Molly still exists for me, though, today, in a form other than the physical. It is almost everything I need, this sense that she is beside me here on the dock, guiding me through the morass of my memory, stepping me over the land mines.

I walked in a fugue, the world clicking past me. I stepped into the gas station's restroom and found myself face to face with a monster: I was cut just below my left eye, a deep gash that spilled blood down the length of my cheek, and then down my neck before finally drying along the line of my clavicle. My thumbnails were ripped down to the very quick in jagged cords, as if they'd been pried out of something solid, something moving, something resisting. My shirt was ripped along the chest and arms.

I'd never believed myself to be a violent person, had never thought that I was more than just a curse to the people who'd loved me, had never stared at myself in a mirror and wondered whose blood laved me.

I cleaned myself off in the bathroom, wadded up and threw away my bloodied shirt and then went back to my car and tried to piece together where I'd been and what I'd done. I listened to the messages on my cell phone and heard only Ginny's voice, telling me to hurry up with my papers so that we could go out and live a little.

It was a weekend. A Sunday. Yes. Why wasn't I in Los Angeles? A rational person would have known that first thing, but I wasn't rational, never had been. An accident? A fight? I concentrated on the pain in my body, tried to localize the suffering, tried to recall the exact events of the previous evening, but there was nothing, only spots of blackness and the stickiness on my hands.

"I remember now," I say.

Bruce shakes his head once and then breathes in deeply. "Paul," he says, "Molly never said anything about you coming up to visit her that weekend. Did she know you were coming?"

"Yes," I say. "Of course she did. It was important!"

"Had you come up before?"

Yes, I think. Every year. "I don't know."

Sheriff Drew's boat is getting closer and I can make out three figures on board. Poor Ginny, I think. She never had a chance.

"I want you to think real hard about what might have happened," Bruce says. "I was with Molly on the anniversary. I spent the night and went back across in the morning. She was alive when I left, Paul."

"This can't be happening," I say, but I know that indeed it can, that I am capable of things.

I walk the length of the dock and try to reconcile myself with a memory that refuses to exist. Yes, I must have hurt her. I tell myself that I must have driven up through California, Oregon, Washington, as I had so many times before, in a sleepless drip of space. I must have watched her from my perch in the woods as she walked through the house in cut-off jeans and a tank top. Must have seen her dusting the living room, pausing over pictures of Katrina, holding the picture to her lips, kissing it. I must have seen her speaking to the picture, telling Katrina how much she missed her, how one day they'd be together again. She must have stood in the kitchen and boiled water for tea, hummed a song just beneath her breath, and dabbed at her eyes. It had been three years since our daughter had passed, an anniversary of despair. I must have circled the house, feeling bolder than I ever had, feeling like today of all days I had to be near the only person who mattered to me. Yes, I tell myself. Yes, this is exactly what happened. I must have stood in the shadows and watched Bruce stumble down the dock, the stench of alcohol slipping from his pores, from the air he exhaled when he crossed right beside me, never feeling my presence because I was no longer opaque, had transformed into another kind of beast altogether.

"I saw you walking down the dock," I say. "You were drunk and you could hardly walk. You were wearing a baseball cap. I remember that. You and Molly argued."

"That's right," he says. "We were fighting about you."

I try to imagine what Molly's life might have been like with Bruce Duper. I imagine them speaking, holding each other, making plans. It would have been good for Molly to live with him. He would have made her happy, I think, and she deserved that.

I must have listened to Bruce and Molly argue at the door, must have seen how they loved each other, knew that time and consequence had finally converged, that there were no more words to describe suffering in my lexicon, no more symbols or formulas to delineate guilt and innocence in matters of the heart. Katrina was gone, Molly was lost to me forever, another person had claimed her, made her his, had experienced emotions that belonged to me alone. I must have heard Molly invite Bruce in, listened as she quietly closed and latched the door, waited until the lights were turned off in the bedroom before I slid in the backdoor and through the rooms of my former life, pausing to smell the wood floors, touching the walls, letting the house melt into me, trusting my habitat. I would have closed my eyes in the darkness of the living room and heard Molly and Bruce sleeping, living. I would have known there were no more chances in this world. While I was an animal capable of great care and concern, I'd reached a terminal point.

"I watched you sleep," I say. I pace back to the end of the dock and stand beside Bruce. "I snuck in the house and watched you and Molly in bed."

Sheriff Drew's voice radiates across the water from a bullhorn on his boat. *"Stay right there! Bruce, keep him right there!"*

Yes, I think, I must have walked into Molly's bedroom and seen her in bed with Bruce Duper; must have looked at her sleeping body like a preying mantis looks at its mate after sex. I must have wanted to devour her, to make her part of me forever.

"The next morning," I say, "I heard you tell Molly to get rid of me. You were holding papers in your hand. Do you remember that?"

"I do," Bruce says sadly. "They were court papers. She'd filed for divorce but had never mailed them to you. She thought they'd put you over the edge."

"They would have," I say. They have. They are.

"Do you know where she is, Paul?"

"I couldn't hurt her," I say. "Could I?"

I can't imagine what I must have done to her. There is not a way for me to quantify what I know must have occurred. I have seen rage throughout the annals of history, yet have no concept how it would manifest itself in me.

The truth, however, is that man has a rich history of brutalizing the ones he loves.

I must have spent that night in the woods planning, thinking, devising. I must have waited until he'd left, reasoned that my anger was not at Bruce but with Molly. The biggest mistake Bruce had made was loving a woman he couldn't completely have. He had started to drink because of it. I had forgotten how decent he was, how honestly he'd lived, how perfect and amiable his existence was without her.

Maybe I walked back inside and smelled him in the folds of the drapes, in the hemlock cones and the cedar leaves and had gone into the kind of rage only a man like myself can: a blind destruction that empties the very corridors that I'm only now able to see.

As I stand beside Bruce Duper's bearlike frame, I admire him, his courage to take a chance with Molly, no matter the consequence. Even if the truth were that she'd never know him as perfectly as she knew me, he was willing. He was willing to do anything to satisfy his desire.

"I'm proud that you loved my wife," I say.

"Where is she?" Bruce says, grabbing me now by the arms. I can smell his anger, can taste it in the back of my throat. "Where did you put her?"

"I don't know," I say.

The human brain decides so much for you: it can black out entire childhoods; it can swallow years of adulthood. Perhaps my brain has done what it has always done: turned the traumatic into silken strips of memory. Love and anger, like science and religion—or even illness—are often guided by arbitrary factors. In the end nothing is natural, every known variable can have a separate unknown. Once you step outside your own life and examine the world, everything seems like something you settle on, a paralyzing addition and subtraction that never quite computes.

EIGHTEEN

I CAN'T BE sure what I believed after I came back to L.A. three weeks ago, because it is still lost to me. Perhaps Ginny knows. Perhaps she can tell me what to believe about myself, because I remember being happy to see her. I remember thinking that I was on a path toward life on a grander scale, that I'd actually become happy, had finally become something other than what I am. Perhaps for the briefest of times I was beautiful: a complete human who could go on living his life, could keep up the pretenses that days, weeks, years of his life hadn't completely dissipated.

"Is she in the woods?" Bruce asks. "You buried her, didn't you?"

"Keep him still," Sheriff Drew shouts. I turn and see him there in his boat and I think that my endings and my beginnings are all the same; that they are ripples in the fabric of my life that crash again and again on the same shore. "Be a gentleman now, Paul. Everything is going to be fine. We're going to get this all settled."

His words are like sediment in my mind. Sheriff Drew runs after me in the forest, back down this very dock. Molly shouts for me just to stop, please stop. And here I come with my girl in my arms, sprinting past where I stand now and diving into the water, my body twisting, turning, sinking to the bottom.

"No," I say to Bruce. "I did not bury her. I know exactly where she is." Bruce's eyes widen and I feel his grip on my arm tighten. "She has always been right here."

Sheriff Drew steps off his boat followed by Ginny and Leo. I hear Ginny's voice, but I cannot make out her words for the roaring in my ears. At some point Ginny will understand that I was incapable of being more than who I am. Maybe, at that point, she'll forgive me for what I've taken from her.

The truth is, I'm saved.

Sheriff Drew walks toward me with his palms up. "Just stay right there. Everything is going to be fine. Just stay where you are."

The truth is that I never was meant to live.

I must have hurt her. I must have brought her back here, to this dock. I must have done for her as I tried to do for Katrina. I must have tried to bring her back.

"I hurt my wife," I say.

"We know, Paul," Sheriff Drew says. I take a step backward and the sheriff moves his hand toward his gun. "Easy there. Easy."

"I know where she is," I say.

"Hold him, Bruce," Sheriff Drew says.

I tilt my head back and feel the breeze off the lake and think that this is the moment I've waited for my entire life.

"Baby," Ginny says. "Stop moving, please!"

I turn and look at Bruce to let him know that it's okay, that I've found the love of his life as well, that we all can be put to rest, but his face is somehow gone—blank—missing even the smallest hint of humanity.

I take another step and Bruce releases me. I'm floating in the air, surrounded by glory, and I'm no longer afraid, no longer confused. For the first time in my entire life, I know who I am, know where I'm going, and maybe I'll come back one day or maybe I'll drift into the ether. Maybe I'll be born into another life in another time.

The water rushes up around me as I sink. Yes, I think, this is what I have always deserved; I am going back to the water, back to knowing peace. I open my eyes to see it, to see everything I've done wrong, to understand that death is but a necessary step.

And I find her.

Beneath the dock, Molly is wrapped in a comforter we purchased two days before Katrina was born, and is weighed down by our old Evinrude engine, an engine Jersey Simpkins had sold us, even when he knew it was temperamental.

An engine I saw when I was here three weeks ago, attached to our boat.

An engine Molly said Bruce Duper took care of.

An engine that Bruce Duper told me he'd removed from our Whaler.

I scream and all the air in my lungs rushes out and I know that it couldn't have been me. I flail away at the water and know that I have tied my life to memories that never existed.

Bruce Duper has killed my wife and buried her beneath my dock.

Molly's hair fans out and dances in the current and for a moment I think that everything is perfect, that Molly is as beautiful now as she will ever be. I crane my head back and stare at the surface of the lake. The sun cuts serrated lines through the water and then I am rising into the sun, my body pulled toward the surface.

"Help me get him up," Sheriff Drew screams.

I feel arms around my chest, under my shoulders, pulling my arms.

"Get him onto the dock."

Ginny and Leo yank me out of the water and lay me flat on the wooden slats.

"She's down there," I say.

"Sit him up," Sheriff Drew says and Leo pulls me forward. The horizon rises and dips before me and I think that maybe I am hallucinating all of this, or that I'm asleep somewhere and that I will wake up in another world.

"He pinned her down with our Evinrude."

"What?" Sheriff Drew says. "What are you saying?"

I turn and look for Bruce and find him standing beside me, staring motionless into the water. "On the Whaler," I say, pointing toward my boat. "He put that Johnson on, see? She's pinned under the dock, Sheriff. He pinned her under the dock with our Evinrude."

"Calm down," Leo says. "Okay? We'll get this sorted out."

Sheriff Drew walks over to the Whaler and inspects the engine. "God damn," he says. "That's a brand new engine. Bruce, is that true? Did you put this engine on her boat?"

"She was all alone out here," Bruce says quietly, his back still turned to the sheriff. "You would have done the same thing, Morris."

"When did you buy this engine?" Sheriff Drew asks.

"I don't recall," Bruce says.

"I didn't kill her," I say to Ginny. "I never hurt her." Ginny brushes hair from my eyes and I see that she is frowning, that her face is older now, smaller, and for a moment I'm not sure I'm seeing anything, not sure my eyes are even open.

"Paul was here constantly, you know that, Morris." Bruce turns around and faces the sheriff and I see something change in him, see a difference in his posture, see that the animal is gone from him, has left him with a cracking shell. "We used to find his footprints in the dirt, used to hear him talking to himself out in the trees. All I did was change out an engine, Morris. That's all I ever did."

"I'm sure that's right," Sheriff Drew says. He's walking slowly toward Bruce now, his gait easy and familiar and I think that I have seen this before, a few days ago, as he came to question me. "But a man starts drinking too much, that affects him, doesn't it? You'd agree with that, wouldn't you, Bruce? You remember how your father got, don't you? Now just tell me when it was you bought that engine and we can all get out of here. Safe and sound."

Bruce stares at me and I think he wants to cry, wants to sit down beside me and weep for a woman neither of us could have, his love for her useless now. He isn't a bear at all. He is human as much or as little as I am.

"She was already dead," Bruce says. He is looking at me but talking to the sheriff. "You know that? She was a ghost. I wanted to help her. I wanted to make her see things."

"You could have," I say.

"All we wanted was for you to be out of our lives," Bruce says. "All I ever wanted was to be hers alone."

"You don't have to say anything else, Bruce," Sheriff Drew says. "You've got rights."

"Why couldn't you have just stayed away?" Bruce says. "Why couldn't you change? You had the chance. You had every chance."

"She is all I ever wanted," I say.

GINNY WALKS ME back into my house while Leo and Sheriff Drew take Bruce across the lake. She lays me down on the bed and rests her hands soft against my face. Less than fifty yards away, Molly waits for me.

"Will they bring her back up?" I say.

"Of course, Paul," Ginny says. "People are on the way right now. Just be still for me, okay baby?"

"Will they make her beautiful again?"

"Whatever you want," she says. She leans in and kisses me on the forehead, and I realize for the first time what it feels like to have a friend, to have someone who loves you despite it all. "Just be still for me."

I close my eyes and Molly is there.

She is asleep on the couch in the living room.

A fire burns in the hearth and the room smells like smoke and hemlock cones. I sit down beside her and put my hand on her cheek. Her skin feels smooth and warm and she opens her eyes and says that she was dreaming of me, that we were back in college.

I lift her up from the waist and hold her close, her body is so warm, and I kiss her hair and I tell her to go back to sleep, baby, just sleep. I stroke her neck and along her back and I whisper that she is as beautiful as the first time I ever saw her, that her lips are like velvet, that she has never been less than the greatest part of my life, that we'd always have time to dream, that I'm sorry, that we would always find a place to love each other, that I'd never stop.

I kiss her forehead and her cheeks and her lips and her neck and I know she is dead and that I am lost, and I kiss her mouth again and say take care of our babies, tell them that I love them, that they are blessed, that they have nothing to be afraid of. Just sleep, baby, just sleep. I'm going to hold you forever, until time doesn't matter, until we are nothing but dust, until the earth, the sun, the moon are gone and there is no memory of us. I will still hold you.

I set her back down on the couch and stare long into her face. She is asleep again, but already she's begun to change, so I take her face into my hands once more and run my thumb over her eyes and say that we wasted so many moments on madness, that all I wanted to do was sit in our clearing in the forest beneath the sunshine talking about the future, holding on to each other, rocking back and forth, never giving up hope, never letting go of the truth, and she was asleep and I crawled in beside her and pressed myself close to her, until I could only hear her breath, could only feel her heartbeat, and I know I can't bring her back. And then she's sitting up and smiling and we are holding hands and it's ten years ago and we are children, just kids, dumb in love and happy. And then I know that I'm in shock, that nothing is right, that I've found the truth, that I found my wife, that truth is slipping, that I am slipping, that Molly's slipping, that she's gone, that we're gone.

Acknowledgments

I AM INDEBTED to the many wonderful people who helped make the publication of this book possible. Foremost, I wish to thank *uber*-agent Jennie Dunham, who tells me and tells me but never says I told you so, for her in-depth reconstruction of this novel; Tom Filer for his passion, wisdom, and honesty; Judi Farkas for her unyielding faith and belief in my work and her uncanny ability to get it in the right hands; Mary Yukari Waters who told me to ground it and then I'd be on to something; All of Goat Alley for suffering through the rough drafts and the false starts and for telling me everything I didn't want to·hear and, certainly, Juris Jurjevics for shepherding this book and for having confidence enough to change it, and to publish it.

Grateful thanks are also due to: Greer Hendricks, for her gentle guidance the first time around and her continued advice; Peter Handel for his sage publicity and baseball acumen; Mom, Lee, Karen, and Linda—my multi-talented family of writers and artists—for career, legal, and Internet advice coupled with never ending love and reinforcement; AJ and Brenda Holcomb, my second set of parents; Todd Harris, always the second reader of the finished product and always my first friend; Jim Kochel, official tour trouble shooter, advance man and source of comedic inspiration; Steve Nitch, whose insight into the human mind was almost as invaluable as his friendship; The Writers' Program at UCLA Extension and all of my students.

It is with great affection that I thank Nana and Papa Dave for bringing us all to The Lake. Much of this was written while remembering the precious hours Papa Dave spent on the water with me talking about life and death and about what happens to the people you love. I wish he were here to see this.

Finally, I am blessed by Wendy. I wrote this book for you.